BRENDAN CONNELL

JOTTINGS FROM A FAR AWAY PLACE

THIS IS A SNUGGLY BOOK

Copyright © 2015 by Brendan Connell
All rights reserved.

ISBN 978-1-943813-01-8

Artwork photography by James Hart.

Brendan Connell

JOTTINGS FROM A FAR AWAY PLACE

Brendan Connell was born in Santa Fe, New Mexico, in 1970. His works of fiction include *Unpleasant Tales* (Eibonvale Press, 2010), *The Architect* (PS Publishing, 2012), *Lives of Notorious Cooks* (Chômu Press, 2012), *Miss Homicide Plays the Flute* (Eibonvale Press, 2013), and *The Metanatural Adventures of Dr. Black* (PS Publishing, 2014).

JOTTINGS FROM A FAR AWAY PLACE

OBSERVATIONS

1. Each of the azimuths and the ecliptic divisions has its own affinity with the elements. Certain entities (huge bellies balanced on thin legs) smile in absolute contentment, being able to live out their days in such style.

2. When Galba was young he had elephants trained to walk the tightrope. Years later, a money-changer was brought to him, accused (maybe falsely) of having cheated a client. He ordered that the man's hands should be chopped off and nailed to his counter. So it is that silly men can often become the most cruel, and they are the ones who generally end up in positions of power.

3. In Shanxi Province, beneath the clouds of coal smoke and wafted by the smell of sulfur dioxide, sits the White Peony Temple. Not looking like much, it was put together with water and moon, back when the rivers and lakes were free, and drunkenness was considered a virtue.

Alan Li Po was a dedicated student of Taoism. He had mastered the mysteries of the cock and hen and studied diligently the *Book of Changes* as well as the *Upper Chapters on the Basic Endeavor*.

Elixial method:

> Outside is an unstable pearl
> Inside: statue of common man

So Alan nurtured his seed and kept his bamboo hidden, prizing peace and cultivating equanimity. When people came, he ran away; when he heard sounds, he remained silent. This is like some wizard drumming and swaying. Taking from Kan, in order to fill up Li.

He dined on pine needles and atractylis root and drank earth juice and an extract of melon seeds.

This is called finding the way. And, finding the way, he was transported six thousand leagues up, on a large puff of pink smoke (non-toxic). It was like a phoenix galloping through the sky.

He felt dizzy, but smiled adequately, soon coming to a huge white palace. Around its summit swam cranes. At its door stood a man. This is how he looked:

> On his head a XXX Beaver
> His stout body wrapped in a purple robe
> White hair on head and crow's feet near eyes
> Mark him as a rodeo immortal

"I'm the Heavenly Worthy of the Numinous Treasure."

"You look familiar," Alan Li Po said uneasily.

And indeed, with his large white moustache, prominent gut and subdued smile, the man did seem familiar.

"Well," the other drawled, "you might have seen me in my previous incarnation. I played Ben Fairchild in *The Ballad of Cable Hogue* and deputy Lon Dedrick in *One-Eyed Jacks*."

"Ah, Mr. Slim Pickens!" Alan said, smiling the smile of the fundamentally pure.

"None other. But like I said, up here they call me Heavenly Worthy of the Numinous Treasure. Don't quite roll off the back of the pick-up as easily, but I'll be damned if I don't like it all the same."

"Most certainly," Alan said, kow-towing three times.

"But you're here to see the boss."

"If I could!"

Mr. Pickens led Alan Li Po down a vast hallway which was paved with jade and lined with huge urns decorated with images of peacocks and chrysanthemums and then through double doors that were about thirty feet high.

The chamber was filled with mist and a subtle but impressive green light.

A man was seated on an ivory throne. On his right stood Lao Tzu, and on his left Chuang Tzu. The former stroked his beard; the latter bowed his head.

Li Po recognized the two Tzus, but not the man in the center.

"That's Hank Williams," Heavenly Worthy Pickens

said. "He's God. When he drinks, he drinks from the big dipper, and he only eats the kernels of stars."

Alan Li Po threw himself on his hands and knees and thrust his forehead to the ground.

"Serve him some celestial yellow dew wine," Hank Williams said. "And get him off the floor."

Immediately a bald young man came out with a jug of wine and a glass and served Alan three cups, one for Tao, one for Heaven, and one for Earth. Han Hsiang-tzu, the patron saint of musicians, came out playing on a flute. Elsewhere, bells, gongs and musical tigers were sounded.

"Your fishing pole was broken, but now it's okay," Williams said, tapping his feet as he listened. "Your creek was filled with sand, but now clear water can flow freely."

It was like a man throwing away pearls, so as not to be robbed.

What a relief!

In fact, Alan Li Po was filled with a great clarity. He could remember five thousand years before when, planting stone seeds on Endless Mountain, he had grown a jade forest and, another time, when he had been born with nine-foot legs and could leap over rivers and tall walls.

"I have heard of your great fame," he said to Hank Williams, "but until today never had the good fortune to meet you. Now that I am here, I humbly ask that you take pity on me."

"Set him up," Williams said, making a friendly motion with his right hand.

Chuang Tzu handed Alan a Silvertone guitar and Lao Tzu handed him a book.

"Is this the *Book of Songs?*" Alan asked.

"Yes, Hank's," Heavenly Worthy of the Numinous Treasure said.

"Learn 'em," Williams advised, "and pluck on the guitar without rest or sleep for five years and even ghosts will become intoxicated with happiness and be rootie tootie, and crocodiles will even carry you across their streams."

After this, Alan Li Po was deposited back on earth.

He immediately began cultivating himself, playing the guitar and diligently studying the book. He refrained from eating grain and began to chat with carp, who gave him lessons in steadfastness.

After three months his fingers had the dexterity of dragons. After a year his voice had the sweetness of jade juice. After three years his playing was like wind and lightning and after five even the Star Gods were impressed.

He left White Peony Temple and wandered about, from mountains to sea coast, from great city to small town. He played in Datong and Chengdu and the people were greatly attracted by the novelty of his style. Some listened, their eyes filled with tears. Others swayed their bodies to the sound.

One night, in the coastal town of Bohai, he began to sing *Honky Tonkin*, and the mollusks on the rocks all grew three legs and began to dance the sugar foot walk.

On another occasion, when he was at the Yu Yin Club in Changchun, his playing caused all in the audience to change sex. The women became men and the men women. All danced in delight and later those present gave birth to small dragons.

The sun and moon chase each other in the sky. When mist is fanned by Heaven, rainbows are raised.

When he was playing in Kunming, there were many rich people present in the audience.

One man, Wang Ka Yan, chairman of AoXing PetroChemicals Ltd., requested that he play *Take These Chains from My Heart*. Alan complied, but when he reached the line *Be as fair to my heart as you can be*, the heads of all the wealthy people came off their shoulders and began to fly around the city, using their ears as wings. A woman who lived on Dongfeng Alley, and who was mopping her floor, put a bucket over one and it was unable to return to its owner.

Three times, CCT, China's leading media station, asked him to come and perform, but each time he refused.

Then one day he disappeared into the hills. It was whispered in the villages that he went to paradise. But sometimes, deep in the night, in the most remote parts of Ningxia and Heilongjiang, when the cattails are meditating on emptiness or the snow is bestowing itself on old tree trunks, a voice can be heard singing:

As we journey along, on life's wicked road,
So selfish are we, for silver and gold,
You can treasure your wealth, your diamonds and gold,
But my friends, it won't save, your poor wicked soul.

4. A man was awoken by some sounds coming from his kitchen. Frightened, he took up a pistol and proceeded to see what the noise was all about. In the kitchen two men were chopping each other up finely with long knives. He shot them, but afterward found out that they were not men after all, but dice.

HABITUALLY DANCING

1. Don't be too exact. Sloppiness makes excellence.

2. Snowy nights are for drinking alone. Hot days are for walking alone. I love to talk. I can talk to walls and rabbits. The same old stories. Please listen.

3. He knocked on the door. A few moments later it creaked open slightly. He slipped into the building. In the dim yellow light he could make her out: an excessively short figure in a dirty pink nightgown. A huge skull out of which sprouted a thin crop of wiry black hairs, large glassy eyes, bosom a shapeless mass, an odor of sweat and vomit issuing from her person.
"Oh Teresa," he cried out in excitement, and then kissed her so deeply that he could almost taste her heart.

4. She had sat in his room since he could remember and kept at bay those things which frighten and kept

watch over the hours of sleep. The gilded flesh of her, masked by robes of white and sealed with eyes serene. The mother of God, or a presumably just representation, cast in plaster and yearning for devotion. A naïve piece of art, yet not devoid of the lambency of life, its truths, and able to cast shadows, or blackest lies.

Elon knelt before her and said his bedtime prayers. God was good and had brought him that far, untainted by the lickerishness of the world and free of the shackles of hate and temptation.

She would guide him and be his pillow, provide a soft place for the young creature to lay his head. The world might roar outside his window, the city where he lived shiver to pieces, yet he would feel the protection of the righteous, the stupidity and innocence of the embryo.

The sheets were soft and vestal white, the mattress stiff and clean. He climbed in and set his limbs in perfect comfort, turned off the light and closed his eyes. The room was black aside from the stripe of moonlight, which slashed through the window and fell upon her, the mother, he thought, of God.

5. There was once a giant bird that nested on the top of a high cliff. Its eggs were very precious, having remarkable aphrodisiac properties.

A certain young man, who was in excellent physical condition, climbed up to get one. He reached the top, grabbed hold of an egg, but then fell down off the cliff and died.

6. There is a certain kind of herb that, if eaten continuously for many years, will make your fingers grow as much as three feet.

7. He was the son of Mygon, King of Phrygia.
He was almost a giant, very handsome and very strong. He would stand by the seashore all day long counting the waves as they came in, wondering how many there were.

8. The stamp of her was on his mind. It was a keyhole and he searched through his pockets in order to unlock that door. The sign of the vulva, existing in the stardust and pitch of space, and he, Elon, was a suitable candidate for that complex.

9. The thick yellow smoke of frankincense wound before her and with palms pressed together he fervently prayed. He decked her with glass beads and rubbed her body with the fat of a dead pig, then the blood of his lips. He yearned to be whipped and beaten with love.
The eyes, of nerveless malachite, looked on with the chill of snow. Let his red blood drip on the ice of her favors, to be frozen into bullets impregnated with pain. He lay prostrate, clawing the floor with perverse and spasmodic joy.

10. Out into the world he went, in search of the ugly.
A long cigarette dripped from his mouth and, as he walked, he kept close to the walls and their shadows and

the stink of their cracks. Hair grew from his face, the hair of the male, and the tender and succulent flesh of the child lay buried in the past. Dead were the days of roses. The way lay littered with thorns, which stung and made the man-creature bridle with that longed-for agony. Little hunchbacks he found and midgets possessed. The woman, her face scarified from who knew what, an object fit for genuine compassion, with thinning hair, a cauliflower nose and eyes dim with pus. He inflamed her and made oblations at the temple of shame, multiple attacks on the scarcely guarded redoubt. The gasping pot of her mouth made him boil from the soles of his feet upward, a surge of morbid satisfaction suscitating his brain.

Dumb cruelty possessed his every action and his lust was steeped deep in hate and rancor. Life became a lascivious parade and no dweller of the street corner was safe from his gripping hands and menu of fetishes.

Elon's beard came to a point like a spike. His eyes were haloed with a sick red, like the skin on the neck of a dead chicken. The heady odor of the whore clung to his person and he walked with predatory, marionette steps. His hair was slicked back, glossy as a griddle. Hot wind erupted from his inflamed nostrils as he muttered obscenities into his shirtsleeve.

11. The statuette stood enshrined and glistening with unknown unguents. A shadowy ghost of her naked self played around her, squatted, and pointed to the secret place. He, with tentacle-like fingers, stroked the wooden

crucifix that dangled from his neck and looked on, prayers issuing from his livid lips. She came, extracted the red and white fluid from him, and left, leaving his emptied skin in her wake.

SHOWING THE WORLD

1. Two sick moles lie under the surface, struggling for breath, thin and depressed, unable to root mountains down or hear lizards sing.

"Why?"

"Because people have found happiness in rushing around, have found beauty in withered things, and have found pleasure in killing even what they don't see."

2. There was a man who was very famous. He ate a great deal of poison.

The previous sentence is sad. Now read the conclusion:

His spirit flew to Clear Jade Terrace and was transformed into a being called Universal Beauty Silver Sage.

If you want to know the adventures of this being, walk as far as you can away from the city.

3. "Look where you will," von Brandt, High Director of Building and Master Exceptional Castle Builder, said

pompously, "you will not find another like it in all of your territories."

The mirrors and statues had been installed, the fresco-painters had done their work decorating the halls and bedchambers with mythological scenes in fleshy pink, milky orange and subdued blue, and now, finally, the place was ready.

Prince-elector Maximilian Wilhelm, Hochmeister of the Teutonic Knights, took a pinch of snuff.

"Yes, you have done well. Standing here, in this delightful embrasure, gazing over the green valley below, neatly divided by that swerve of river, I feel a sensation of satisfaction. It is always pleasant to install oneself, to spend a night in a new castle."

That evening von Brandt sat at the prince-elector's table, ate well and drank more claret than could be recommended. The next day he awoke with a headache. After being dressed by his valet, a young man with a very long neck and a very short nose, he left his room and made his way down the great staircase. The prince-elector stood by a window in the great hall.

"Von Brandt," he said in measured tones of superiority, "I thought you told me that this palace you built me was unique."

"And so it is."

"Then what, pray tell, is that structure I see across the valley?"

The architect, placing himself before the window, raised his monocle to his right eye and looked before him. Indeed, just opposite, he saw a castle exactly identical to the one he had built, the one in which he now stood.

"Very curious," he murmured. "It must be some sort of optical illusion."

"It is anything but," Maximilian Wilhelm said peevishly. "I have returned from there not ten minutes since, and I can guarantee you it is a structure of stone and mortar exceptionally identical to this one."

"But it was not there yesterday!"

"But it is today."

"It took us over twelve years to build this palace."

"Well, there seems to be someone in the neighborhood able to work a bit more quickly than yourself."

Though the day was one of brilliant sunshine it was, for both the prince-elector and his architect, one of gloom. The former brooded about the falconry and stables, had a servant caned, and was especially cold toward his consort. The latter strode around the premises of the new structure, an adequate level of astonishment displayed on his features as he noted that the thing was, detail for detail, a precise replica of his own creation, from the onion-shaped towers to the chandeliers of Meissen porcelain which he perceived when he peeked through the windows.

That evening von Brandt had trouble sleeping. It seemed to him that the walls of his chamber were distending, the ceiling higher. He dreamt that he was being suppressed beneath the heavy end of a moss-covered stone.

As dawn stretched fat white arms over the countryside, he climbed out of bed and, still in his night clothes, peered out the window, letting out an exclamation which was not to be found in any of the treatises of the great Johann Christoph Gottsched. For he now saw three castles—that from the day previous, and two new ones—each exactly identical.

He stepped back and curled his toes, whistled loudly through his nostrils, went to his valet's chamber, which was near at hand, kicked him, and demanded to be dressed on the instant.

A quarter of an hour later he was in the great hall, face to face with the prince-elector, who met him with a bitter smile.

"Observe the new tenants," the prince-elector remarked.

Through the circle of his monocle, von Brandt could make out a group of peasants, accompanied by a cart laden with blankets, pots, a cage of live chickens, four ducks, and a lazy dog, making their way into one of the castles.

"This will not do," Wilhelm said. "I cannot have every maker of butter living in the same style as myself."

At around noon the next day, just as lunch was being served, a carriage sped madly up the hill and stopped before the prince's palace.

A footman opened the door and a fat, somewhat elderly gentleman in a white wig descended. The palace doors swung open for him as if by magic and he was shown directly before the prince-elector.

"Ah, De Vrunt, finally you are here."

"You called; I came."

18

Nibbling on a chicken wing, the prince explained the problem.

"Yesterday there were three castles. Today there are six. Poor rascals are being attracted from all about and are setting up house in plain view. And I am so tired of being annoyed."

"I will investigate," De Vrunt, Chief Surveyor of the Royal Household (Terrestrial, Astral and Microscopic) said gravely.

Shortly before the dinner hour the great scientist reappeared. Opening his hands so the palms were turned upward, he spoke.

"My good Prince, I have studied the problem, that is, I have visited all the neighboring specimens, and have reached a conclusion which, as extraordinary as it may seem, can nonetheless be verified with mathematical precision, in the same way that, by observing the red spot (first noted by Cassini) on the planet Jupiter, it can be deducted that the said astral body is in a constant flurry of rotation;—so, though *entia non sunt multiplicanda praeter necessitatem*, it would seem that your castle is reproducing itself and, in fact, if left unchecked, will continue to do so exponentially."

"Your suggestion?"

"They must be destroyed—all of the castles, including your own, must be destroyed."

"But I have just moved in."

"*Surgit amari aliquid*, my Prince, *surgit amari aliquid*. If you leave this unfortunate structure to do its vile and extra-organic work, the peasantry will no longer be peasantry. Natural order will be disturbed. Not only will this building lose all intrinsic value, but the other palaces and castles you have scattered across the kingdom will become worthless as well, and your very lifestyle put in the utmost danger. Wealth is only appreciated due to its rarity."

The prince-elector shivered and, after touching his forehead with the fingers of his right hand, as a pampered gentleman does when he feels somewhat dizzy, gave his royal consent.

At once was General von Haufhauser sent for and the next day he came, bringing with him his great blond moustache, a thousand men carrying pikes and blunderbusses, several hundred dragoons, and numerous machines for war. Commands burst forth from his lungs. He raced on horseback from one end of the valley to the other, bouncing in his saddle, waving his saber, the grass being torn up under the iron-shod hooves of his horse.

Cannons were planted on the summit of a hill. The prince-elector and his household were asked to abandon his establishment. A tent was set up for him near a large oak tree and he was served a glass of Burgundy.

A trumpeter let out a cry, while a young man with a long chin beat a drum. A few men on horseback galloped from castle to castle shouting for the inhabitants to leave and disperse themselves.

The peasants, hearing the noise, came out; seeing the forces, many of them scattered, looks of terror on their faces. Some, however, remained, not so ready to give up their new and luxurious homes at the first sign of trouble.

"Why should we leave?" a pig farmer said. "These buildings are empty."

"That's right," a tanner with a thick beard agreed, waving his fist in the air. "We've been living in hovels long enough. It's time we enjoyed the good life."

It was then that a group of about fifty uniformed men could be seen marching toward them. When they were about one hundred meters away, they stopped and began to load their muskets.

"Hold your ground," the pig farmer shouted bravely.

The soldiers took aim. There was a crackle of fire. A musket ball sallied through a beard. Another, whistling the refrain from Gottfried Finger's Sonata in C major, pushed its way through the brim of a hat.

The peasants, suddenly re-evaluating the true worth of the good life, scattered, loping off into the distance so as to get out of range. A few ducks ran after them. The soldiers shouted.

General von Haufhauser, who had been observing the scene through a pair of double opera glasses, gave orders for the men to withdraw and the cannons to be fired.

Fuses were lit. Cannonballs ripped through the towers, went crashing through high ceilings. The violent boom of the artillery was mingled with a vague moaning, that seemed to come from the buildings themselves.

It was soon time for the general assault to begin.

The men were brave. Their spirits were high.

With huge battering rams they broke down the unlocked doors of the castles and with shovels undermined their foundations. Bits of elaborate stucco work crumbled. The chandeliers of Meissen porcelain shattered, as did mirrors and statues, and mythological frescoes were dissolved.

By late afternoon, great damage had been done. Walls had collapsed, towers fallen to earth. The sun set. The moon came out. The campaign continued, the forces of the general expecting victory at any moment.

By candlelight, the prince-elector was served a plate of cold beef in jelly and a bottle of Champagne. Three dragoons and a page boy stood guard over him. Von Brandt was given half a glass.

"Military expeditions always make me hungry," the Hochmeister of the Teutonic Knights commented, swallowing his food.

Von Brandt muttered something about salt.

Not far distant, General von Haufhauser stood near a roaring bonfire.

A messenger came dashing up to him bearing a note from Lieutenant Velhagen, who was the following week to be married to Helga, beautiful despite her limp.

The general hastily looked over the note.

"New castles have appeared to the south and to the east. We must crush the hostile forces," he said in a determined voice. "We must obliterate them."

De Vrunt appeared. His wig was on lopsided. With wide eyes and in a voice like a half-empty bucket he spoke to the general.

"They are reproducing in a manner not unlike certain woody perennial plants I have observed in the botanical gardens at the University of Padua. If only it were possible to save some specimen to install in the Royal Museum of Paranormality."

"Destroy!" the general shouted, his great blond moustache bristling.

The guns roared. The nearby peasants were rallied to the aid of the army with promises of kegs of butter and came with hoes and picks.

The castles seemed to rumble slightly. It was possible they cried. A horse could be heard neighing wildly in the darkness.

The prince-elector yawned as he observed tongues of flame erupting in the distance. The soldiers and peasants worked together throughout the night, gutting the buildings with fire, razing the structures to the ground one after the next. They scattered dislodged bricks and blocks of stone through the fields.

The morning light revealed a scene of destruction. Smoking ashes and men with charcoal-smudged faces. A thin dog was sniffing about.

Von Brandt's monocle became clouded. A large tear rolled out of his left eye. No longer could he declare himself High Director of Building and Master Exceptional Castle Builder. Maybe he would take up some obscure vocation in order to feed his family. Maybe he would flee to the frontier and abandon them altogether.

Prince-elector Maximilian Wilhelm mounted his horse and rode swiftly back to the capitol, the peacock's feather in his hat waving in the wind.

4. Those who knew the aged woman could not remember when her belly had been anything less than tremendous. It jutted forward, spheroid, seemingly extra-terrestrial.

The doctor was impressed; he prodded,—scalpel in hand, extracted.

To be a mother, even at a ripe age, is delightful.

So it was, as she held the stone foetus in her arms.

ENTRUSTING

1. Once when Bodhidharma was ascending Shaoshi mountain, he passed a boy who was sitting on the side of the path.
"Where are you going?" the boy asked.
"To the top of this mountain to cross my legs and meditate."
"It must be hot up there."
"Why?"
"Because it's closer to the sun."
In his next life the boy was reborn in Bhaisajyaguru's Eastern Paradise.

2. Reports of a distant axe.

3. Emile's grandmother, upon returning from a round-the-world trip, dispensed gifts to the entire family. Though everyone received something interesting, Emile liked his own present best.
"I bought it in the little town of Vrindavan, in India," his grandmother said.

The boy gazed at the statue (for that is what it was) in awe. The figure was around ten inches high, and made of bronze. Black with dirt and somewhat greasy, it seemed old and, for all anyone could tell, was an antique.

"It looks like some kind of demon," said Emile's father, Drummond.

The grandmother raised her eyebrows. "I believe it is an Indian god," she said.

Emile's mother said that the only god she trusted was the one at the Rolling Acres Christian Church. "All those arms and heads frighten me."

Emile put the statue in his room, on a shelf. He offered it water and fruit and then a leg of roasted chicken. The next morning, after climbing out of bed, he bowed to it.

"Praise the Indian god," he said.

The several jaws, filled with tongues and teeth, grinned. Tiger's skin, cudgel, hibiscus-red, primal sound.

When, ten years later, Emile attended Cornell University, in the town of Ithaca, New York, he rented a very small, second-story studio apartment on East Tompkins St. To get to classes in the morning he walked for twenty minutes, along a trail that slipped through the inside of a gorge. The high stone walls were patched with moss and sweated liquid. There was a great waterfall he passed, and the river was full of fish.

When the farmers in the surrounding countryside began to complain about mysterious killings done to their livestock, the matter was generally treated with smiling indulgence. Emile took the livers, usually those of sheep and goats, and placed them on a ceramic plate before the statue. He poured out numerous shots of whisky, being careful not to spill a drop, and placed them in a line before the god. And then, his brain erupting with hot fantasies, he would crawl into his bed, the sheets strewn with tacks, and laying his head upon a shattered pot, would pray in earnest, biting his thumb.

A RAMSHACKLE VILLAGE

1. There were human torsos dangling from thin ropes, being salted and cured for those long winter months, and bottles of fingers and toes being pickled with radishes and greens to provide a tasty hors d'oeuvre when company came to dine.

2. Breakfasted on lambstones.

3. In order for him to assume the position of emperor, he had two thousand eight hundred neighboring lords murdered, including his own brother. For his coronation war, he took five thousand one hundred prisoners for sacrifice. When he returned to his palace, he had the entire staff killed, even those he had smiled and laughed with, because they had seen him in the role of a human.

That first sacrifice was a bloody plenitude. He was adorned with a bright down cape, his legs and arms decorated with dyed turkey feathers. He stood at the top of the sacred pyramid and watched as his followers dragged the victims up the steep steps. Some howled in terror, begging for mercy. Others, those who were not cowards, came forward without argument, ready to meet an honorable finish.

One by one they were tied to the sacrificial table. With a knife made from the sharpened snout of a swordfish, he performed the rites. He plunged the blade into their chests and plucked out their still beating hearts, then held them up to the sun, dripping with blood, as an offering. Laying them on tortillas of corn he consumed them, the warm essence of his enemies sinking into his belly.

The people down below danced and sang, waving their arms in the air. The young men, aroused by the blood, chased the laughing females and pleasure girls off into the jungle.

He had the flesh of his enemies divided amongst his people. The women cooked the meat in large clay vessels and served it, decorated with golden squash blossoms.

Drunk with death, he continued, hour after hour, to participate in the sacrifice. Some, frightened out of their wits, tried to crawl away on all fours, like animals. With these he was particularly vicious, flaying them alive and draping their skins over his back while they looked on, eyes crimson with terror. When he cut open their breasts the blood would gush forth, spurting high in the air, and then relax into a slow gurgle. He rejoiced in this and plucked and consumed the hearts until, exhausted, he could no longer stand, and his stomach protruded, gorged with the fruit of his cruelty.

4. The most refreshing drink some warm pop a pool mother's splashing with their grinning children now kicking a head about a court. We climbed down the wet stone steps. A carved slab behind it another world of underground birds.

5. There was a small village in the mountains where everyone was happy and contented. They did the work they needed to do, which was not a great deal, ate much, and slept more.
    One day a carriage rolled in and out hopped a tall man wrapped in a fur cloak. He carried a cane and walked with long steps.
    From house to house he went, buying up dreams. After that, he left.

GHOST CAVE

1. Fall came with its rain, puddles dimpled and bubbled, stripped tree limbs dripped; and soon winter had set in. Perpetually dark skies and frigid atmosphere; snow piled up. He spent his time indoors, staring out the window at the slush-covered streets.

The endless grey of the sky seemed to kill the restrictions of space, deranging the familiar and acting as an occult backdrop to the shapes of the terrestrial sphere.

He pulled over at a spot he was familiar with. The only other vehicle in the parking area was a truck that stood there idling, cab empty, exhaust streaming from its tail pipe and snow building up on its hood. He got out of his car, erecting the collar of his jacket up over his ears. The trail—during the warm time of year it was pleasant, the pines giving off an intoxicating aroma and the clearings filled with beds of clover and wildflowers that existed drowsily amongst the hum of bees, drifting of butterflies and the surrounding shade of rising hills. A bird would fly from branch to branch. The trail would take on a primeval look, with its root-ridden earth memory of mushroom carbon monocots joined limbs or some segmented worm. But now it was winter. The sparsely falling snow drew pale arabesques in the sky. The trees were leafless. Pines stood mutinous, their snow-crusted limbs taut and cowled, aping, posing.

He walked down the trail, noticed some footprints diverging off to the side, deep solitary prints sunk in the fresh snow. He followed them instinctively. After about fifty yards or so he saw that they led to a bundle. He quickened. A giant backpack or pile of clothes. No footprints led away. Just toward; into. He looked closer and could make out flesh, an upturned shirt, a back. There was a gun in that hand, tight, twisted rigor mortis.

2. There was once a woman in Ecuador who had a child with bells instead of ears. No one knew who the father was.

3. Words aren't precious, but nothing is.

4. A casualty of the age, he marauded, crawled on all fours, became lost, wrung by madness, trauma. He tried to wash mud to make it clean. A tide of stars made the fool drop into dizzying aether an abnormally excited state of mind the grass whipped to one side.

5. If you read this late at night, alone.

GRADUAL ACTIVITY

1. People love to be distracted.

2. Even tears aren't as wet as my mind some liquid eel lodged in the sand panting for rain.

3. One day he looked around and saw that everything was attached by strings. The trees: the tip of each branch had a string attached to it which led to the sky. The ends of his fingers also.
   Grabbing hold of three or four of these, he pulled himself up.

4. Father Wright was considered a model of virtue by his associates. Few men led a more pious, ascetic existence. The stern look of his chiseled features, that deliberate and aggressive swish of his garments, filled other priests with awe. Often he was consulted about sticky textual points, matters of authority. His contemporaries considered him to be the equal of Abbot Pambo, Macarius, or John the Dwarf.

He was very fond of taking on the burden of others' sins. Eagerly, a corner of his mouth faintly twitching, he advanced to the confessional, shutting the little door behind him with actual haste. A troubled soul would darken the grate to ask forgiveness. With rapt attention the embracer of poverty listened, felt mundane breath filter through.

All too often it was some old woman frightened of her own evil thoughts, strands of greed, quaking lest they lead her to grim Hades. As soon as the nature of her dilemma became known, he offered absolution, disdaining even to hear her out, advance the downed creature the opportunity of a proper audience.

And he was hardly more fond of the cheating wife. Seldom would such a being have anything interesting to say, always weeping, whining over the unsanctioned horizontal position. Adultery, in the end, was a rather dry business. Rarely indeed would those lips give utterance to admission of the rollicking orgy, with masks of barkcloth, dressed in raffia—some dance of drama and spirit.

His peccadillo, however, we will not name. A handkerchief he kept handy to wipe the sweat from his vein-marbled forehead. It was all he could do to keep from offering up an enlightenment such as Rousseau, that genius, had experienced at an early age.

The air in his body would issue forth humid and short. Gasping, the man asked for particulars amidst words concerning the cleansing of the soul. He wanted a detailed map of the sensations, a step by step exposé of all the sordid actualities.

After such an occasion his form would stumble forth, face pale and drawn, more severe and ascetic in appearance than ever. With hasty steps he made his way back to his cell; a bare chamber; a chair, a bed and a plain wooden cross.

5. This is a memory I would like to share:
James Frye was an extraordinary man, the best-read man I had ever known. He was like a modern Athenaeus. He could quote from authors both classic and modern. He knew everything about books.

I remember when I first met him. It was in Milan. At the Bar Cowboy. I ordered a Campari Soda, he a white wine.

Or was it the bar Little Boy?

Anyhow, I'm sure it was a beer he was drinking, as the weather was hot. He had a golden moustache and . . .

But wait. His name was not James. No, it was Jerry. I remember quite perfectly, it was Jerry. Jerry Frye.

Actually, he never read a book in his life.

6. When I was a boy, I had a fever. Waking up I heard screaming, but I was alone. Then I began climbing the wall of a canyon, boulders falling all around me.

People do not usually reach the top, but I did.

7. Nothing sounds so good as nothing.

UNCOMMON

1. Dry leaves scrape together as a skunk trots through the darkness.

2. His head shimmering with heat on a black tribune.

3. He could hear their footsteps behind him and their moans at having to go about without sandals—as if sandals could matter at a time like this, when death was on the land. He himself rejoiced in the sackcloth that covered his body and the rough ground under his bare feet. It was little suffering indeed compared to what his people were undergoing; and then he and the elders made their way through the desolate streets of the city. The sound of desperate prayers and weeping could be heard from behind virtually every door—not the mere lackadaisical weeping of lone sorrow, but the shaking, uncontrolled sobs of horror, of panic. A scream shot out from one distant housetop. A dog trotted out from a dusty alleyway, a blue and stiff joint set firm in its mouth. It stopped, looked, and then continued on its way.

As the Shoot of Eshai and his party turned a corner they were greeted by an unpleasant sight. A beggar, long known in that neighborhood, sat against one wall. His breath was slow and wheezing and his eyes exuded a thick, sluggish mucus. His arms and legs were covered with black spots and his neck was expanded to the size of his waist. He could not properly adjust his arms due to the buboes which swelled their pits.

Dead rats lay littering the gutters, fur slick with wet, lips turned back, revealing their sharp, prehensile foreteeth.

Further down the street was a slowly advancing cart, drawn by oxen. The Shoot of Eshai knew it to be one of the carts he had ordered to go about the city. At every door it would stop and the driver and his assistant call out in grave voices: "I AM WHO I AM is eternally merciful!" Upon which there would either be no reply, or the door would open and the two men would be invited in to fetch a corpse, which they would add to the heap on the back of the cart. Those doors from which they had fetched such burdens they would mark with a sign in charcoal, to let it be known that the pest was therein.

The Shoot of Eshai noticed that his companions hurried as they passed the cart, pushing him forward from behind. Undoubtedly the sight both scared and nauseated them. The tangle of blackish-blue limbs, the agonized, lifeless faces still damp with pustulous matter, were enough to make even the most steadfast lose heart.

"They say that some seventy thousand men of Canaan have met this end these three days," whispered one of the elders, his voice shaking, the man obviously on the brink of tears.

The face of the Shoot of Eshai twisted in disgust and shame. Through his desire to count these very men when they lived and breathed, his desire to number, take census of his people, this pestilence had arisen. Without question it was the immortal worm who had burrowed into him and planted this wicked need which so displeased I AM WHO I AM.

Then Gad, the Shoot of Eshai's seer, had brought him word from I AM WHO I AM; a choice of three punishments: three years of famine, three months of war, or three days under the sword of I AM WHO I AM.

"Let me now fall into the hand of I AM WHO I AM," the Shoot of Eshai had said; "for great are his mercies: but let me not fall into the hand of man."

Now, however, as he heard the sobs of husbandless wives behind every other door and saw the plumes of brown smoke rising from the east, smelled the odor of burning flesh, he questioned his own mind. To smell the delicious aroma of roasting chines of beef on the wind had always been his delight, but this other, this vapor infused with the profound suffering of man—it made his stomach turn.

Mastering himself, he pressed close to one of the elders and asked, "So where is the place of this Ornan the Jebusite, where it is said Sariel is hovering?"

"We are not far," the man replied, looking at the Shoot of Eshai with his sad, scared eyes, and then advanced ahead of the rest and humbly led the way.

The air of the town was humid and unsavory and as they walked through the narrow streets and alleyways the charcoal-marked doors became more frequent, until it could be seen that nearly every door was marked this way, with a black sign. The Shoot of Eshai's companions walked with their sleeves over their mouths, as if this would somehow filter out the contamination which was laying low their people, but he did not. He knew, as he saw a man standing at the doorway on one side, groins bleeding, and another, dead, a ghoulish mass of dilated flesh slumped in the frame of a window, that this visitation was due to his own foolishness.

The air grew sticky and extremely difficult to breathe. A few rays of light stole across his path and then disappeared. The sky was smirched with darkness.

"We are approaching the place of Ornan the Jebusite," said the elder who led the way, articulating the words with bleak gravity.

The Shoot of Eshai looked at the threshing floor, the wattle fence surrounding it and the large mud building by its side, and then, raising his head, he saw the apparition. He felt his breath, two hot streams, emit from his nostrils.

It floated, an immense boiling cloud over the threshing floor. Yet, unlike a cloud, it had thickness and substance. Grim, birdlike features dripped from it. An armor of scales, or dark, tar-like feathers, formed an aureole or backdrop. Leashes wound from it like mist, creatures darting dexterously about attached to each: froglike, venomous demons, fanged and bloodthirsty.

The apparition stretched out its limbs and they rolled over the Oasis of Truth, one holding a naked sword which trembled like scales in a balance, the blade of it being weighted down by numerous fiends, impish and frolicking with malice, while the handle was held by Sariel.

The Shoot of Eshai and the elders, each and every one, fell down upon their knees, and set their heads to the dust. With hands clenched white each man raised his voice in pathetic laments, begging the mercy of I AM WHO I AM—for him to cage this roiling force of pain, which, with one clawing touch would set boils erupting and poison the very flesh, making the victims lash themselves mad for the freedom of death.

"I have sinned and done evil," cried the Shoot of Eshai, raising his eyes toward heaven; "but what has the crowd done?"

Then Gad approached the Shoot of Eshai. "Sariel told me," he said in a hoarse, choked voice, "that just as this is the threshing floor of Ornan, so is Canaan the threshing floor of I AM WHO I AM. And the wheat shall be separated from the chaff." And he went on to say how I AM WHO I AM had come to him and whispered in his ear that the Shoot of Eshai should build an altar in the threshing floor of Ornan the Jebusite—an altar for I AM WHO I AM.

The Shoot of Eshai felt the wind of death blow around him and heard it, like the sound of cattle licking up water. He looked and saw Ornan threshing wheat, his four sons standing in the doorway of the house, looking on with terror. And it was as Gad had said. For as the grain was beaten, horrible cries went up in the city round, and it was sure that the devil himself was harvesting a great crop of sinners. The future was dark, seemingly thrust away, and in its place sat unmoving the heavy ball of suffering, and the shrieking living, outnumbered by the dead.

    The Shoot of Eshai approached Ornan and said, "Sell me the location of the threshing floor, at full price. Then I will be able to build an altar."

    "Take it and do what you want with it," Ornan replied, bowing. "And I will give you oxen to burn and you can burn them with my threshing boards and take my wheat too. Take it all."

    "No," the Shoot of Eshai objected; "but I will buy it for the full price. I pay for what I take."

    And so he bought the place from Ornan for six hundred shekels of gold and built an altar to I AM WHO I AM. He had the oxen brought and felled them, on the north side of the altar. They were cut open and the ground made wet, enriched with their blood, which ran like hot bubbling springs, spreading out and being absorbed, as does spilt wine on a carpet. The Shoot of Eshai dipped his fingers in the warm liquid and sprinkled it round about upon the altar, and he then flayed the oxen and cut the meat into pieces. A fire was built upon which he laid the heads, smeared with blood and fat of the rump, taken from the vicinity of the backbone; as well as the fat that covered the inwards. The two kidneys, and the fat that was on them, by the flanks, and the caul above the liver, with the kidneys, were also burnt, to appease the wrath of I AM WHO I AM. The hides, the flesh, and dung of the oxen he burnt upon the altar, and it was a sweet savor for I AM WHO I AM.

The malignant creatures stationed around Sariel flinched, licked their lips and came forward, breathing in the pungent aroma of sacrifice. A yellowish-grey smoke rose from the burning flesh and fat and mingled with the lowering cloud. The flames crackled and rose, consuming the sizzling drippings, and the somewhat rank perfume was dissipated, along with that apparition which sat between heaven and earth, by a brisk wind.

I AM WHO I AM had commanded Sariel, and the sword was again put up in its sheath.

The sun set that evening in a clear orange sky and all was peaceful. The black, spiral trails of those bonfires, which were stationed outside the city, climbed toward heaven and from the houses laughter could be jointly heard with weeping, like flowers springing from ashes. But the Shoot of Eshai was afraid, because of the sword of Sariel.

4. An old man had searched through his life for truth and when he found it cried some beautiful painful thing.

5. All the words in the world can be wrapped in a ball.

DEFILEMENTS

1. The emperor wandered across the courtyard, dragging his scepter through the dust.

Presently, a carriage came, pulled along by four great bony horses. On it hung a large placard, on which the word 'Eternal' was inscribed.

The driver got down, swung his tail this way and that.

"Flavius Petrus Sabbatius Justinianus?" he said.

"Yes, that's me."

"If you would care to go for a ride."

The emperor climbed in the carriage and the horses started off at a trot.

"By the way," the emperor cried out to the driver, "What does that word on the placard mean?"

"The King of Hell put it there. When you arrive in his domain, he will add the word 'Damnation'."

2. "Who is she?"

"They call her Donna Fioretta."

"She is magnificent, like a lily," Fra Bernardo said.

"Though quite unpluckable," commented his clerk, Ugolotto, a young man of oily appearance, bloated as a toad, limy-skinned like a starfish, some creature grown from the castaway milt of the clergy. "They say that she has taken a vow of virginity."

The friar, Fra Bernardo, who was much given to pleasure, scratched his chin and looked over the congregation: a morass of pious old women, dried up maidens, bones protruding from their figures like driftwood on deserted beaches, lips sharp and passionless as the beaks of cormorants; Donna Fioretta rising out of that pile of leached dung, a religious smile, exuding an arousing perfume. Her body, full and beautiful, was the sort to easily make a man forget all other business.

"I will have her," murmured the friar, feeling a putrescent heat, like that of compost, swelling his cassock.

"If you come in the early morning, before the sun rises, you will find her here, praying alone."

"You seem to know her habits well?"

"Certainly," Ugolotto replied with a smirk. "A properly trained hound always smells its master's quarry."

That evening, by the light of three tallow tapers, Fra Bernardo, a student of Fra Giovanni da Fiesole, otherwise known as Beato Angelico, set to work. Mixing urine and malachite he had his dazzling green; the dried petals of irises and ground basalt an astounding blue; jasper and the scales of the *Priacanthus cruentatus* for red. He worked as a man inspired. On numerous slips of paper he painted scenes of concupiscence, the figures marvelously foreshortened, the images irrupting hot as geysers, draperies and positions boldly fashioned. Humans, in their naked state, toppled madly over each other; piles of flesh, like pink sea shells, fell into numerous patterns, positions, encompassing all of those described by Aretino, in his *Sonnetti lussuriosi* and Veniero, in his *Puttana errante*. As a heading to each image, each slip of paper, he wrote the words in purest gold, in characters gorgeous:

> *Fioretta, my righteous daughter, your body has been chosen as the receptacle for this earth's next great apostle. Give yourself to the first holy man you see, and the deed will be pure as the light of heaven, the place from which I look down with consecrating gaze, demanding your absolute obedience.*

The next morning Fioretta entered the church, walking with mincing steps, head bowed in devout modesty. She kneeled, clasped her hands together, gazed up at the dripping wounds and prayed. A slip of paper, like the feather of some exotic bird, a parrot or a peacock, floated down, applying itself, face upward, to the floor before her. She looked down, gathered in the image and felt the blood boil through her breasts and ascend directly upward to her cheeks. With parted lips she read the inscription, her scarlet tongue floating between her teeth. Her spine tingled. She gasped.

Other slips began to descend, drifting like mammoth flakes of painted snow—lubricious and always bearing the same inscription—demanding the receptacle of her body for the gratification of heaven. Rainbows of twisted, lusting limbs, exposed pudenda and phallic compositions were there as the sky dribbled angels and radiated glowing webs of copulation.

She gathered them up, fed on their imagery and let the golden words coax her modesty. She back-stepped, turned and stumbled toward the doors.

Ugolotto let out a croak, a chuckle from his hidden and precarious position above as he saw the young woman run against Fra Bernardo, who just then entered (as planned).

She looked at him with large eyes.

"What is troubling you, my daughter?" he asked, peering hard at her mouth and, though speaking with a firm and pious voice, secretly longing to strangle her organ of speech with his own.

"I have been touched by—by—by—I know not if by God or the Devil!"

She explained; she showed the slips of paper, blushing to the roots of her hair.

"These are most certainly missives from heaven!" Fra Bernardo exclaimed, feigning surprise.

"What should I do, holy man? I am filled with confusion."

"What is it you think you should do?"

"Obey the words of the Lord, the mysterious words of God."

"This seems the most blessed, the most appropriate line of behavior."

"You are the first holy man that I have seen."

"God has willed it so."

"As I am completely ignorant as to how these matters progress, I await your instructions."

"This evening, after the sun has set, come to my chamber and I will perform the sanctified deed, I will show you the arches of paradise."

"The Almighty demands my obedience, father," Fioretta said, and departed, steps unsteady and body fluxing with dangerous sensation.

At home she knelt before a small ivory crucifix and prayed in earnest that she might properly fulfill the wishes of heaven and show herself a worthy receptacle. Her mind, still affected by the images depicted on the slips of paper, was filled with a vague alarm, an overwhelming curiosity concerning the divine mysteries. With hot breath she exhaled her supplications, wanting nothing more than to be an instrument of the Lord.

Fra Bernardo spent the afternoon in preparing his body for the activity of evening, bathing it in perfumed water and rubbing it with oil of rose and oil of olives. He sipped at a bottle of Barbera del Monferrato, a restorative wine from Piedmonte, after which he sent Ugolotto out to fetch him a royal supper from a reputable inn not far distant. For starters he had a swan in chauldron sauce. The gravy, of giblets strained with blood of the bird and a little piece of the liver, cinnamon, ginger, pepper, salt and sugar, was as rich as it was divine. He then ate a chine of beef and a breast of mutton boiled and stewed in claret. This was followed by a pastry of fallow deer, three green geese in a dish with sorrel sauce, a stork in vinegar, and lampreys in yolks of eggs and the livers of stock doves. By dessert, which was a syrup of violets and whole cherries in confection, he felt his manhood primed for any task and could scarcely wait the short time that remained before Donna Fioretta was due at his chamber.

The rays of the sun descended behind the yellow Tuscan hills, which were furrowed, scarred with grape vines, their fruit swelling, ready to burst as with blood; and the friar paced his chamber, feeling the sticky skin of his thighs rub against each other while, under his breath, he chanted rampant psalms. When it grew dark he lit the tapers, and licked, with an agile tongue, the foam from his lips, his fingers touching the weeping shafts. He decked his bed with fleeces, rabbit and goat skins, and then lit in a dish incense of myrrh. He sniffed in the aroma, gazed into the smoke and let his mind traipse across fields of vice.

There was a knock at the door and she entered, Ugolotto pushing her forward into the room. She was dressed charmingly in garments of blue sarcenet which, though hiding her figure, perseveringly alluded to its bold prominences. Her neck pale and cheeks flushed; agitated like a dog ready to rub itself raw in a dirty rut. The friar, upon seeing her so innocently discomposed, felt his desire to possess her redouble.

"Are you prepared to lend your body to this holy task?" he asked.

"As God wills it."

"Let your garments drop."

The shaggy mane and regalia of a wounded sea

creature; the magenta overtures of a shred of flesh.

Holding his breath, he drank in the image with the thirst of hellfire, and, flinging away the mask of good manners, grabbed her up and threw her roughly upon his bed.

"What religion is this?" she cried, feeling his grasp tighten around the fragile stalk of her waist and watching, with wide eyes, how he mounted the pulpit. "What are you doing?"

"In my profession we call this process 'sending the Pope to Rome' and it is believed to be the most sanctified of all earthly acts. Now, open up the door to St. Peter's and let the Supreme Pastor perform his blessed office!"

Donna Fioretta, who was by this time stirred to a state of high reverence, gladly abandoned her defenses in order to let the friar prove his words with deeds. The latter, his nail well tempered in the furnace of desire, proceeded to drive it into her wounds, all the while giving vehement praises unto God and asking the young woman if she was yet prepared to pay homage to the Deity. Feeling herself filled with a new and most blessed sensation, Donna Fioretta screamed out that she was indeed redeemed and wanted nothing more than to witness the righteous fury of the Lord. Fra Bernardo, ever ready to labor for a just cause, called upon heaven to witness the act, whereupon he confirmed Fioretta to a new faith, letting her witness not only the resurrection, and the ascension, but also the coming of the Holy Spirit.

Now, Ugolotto had been listening the whole while at the door, enjoying the melody he heard within and feeling the torture of longing unsettle his brain. Becoming overwhelmed with the most urgent inspiration, he was on the point of privately strumming the strings of his own mandolin, when he became aware that the noise within had almost ceased. He stealthily entered the chamber, where he saw Fra Bernardo fast asleep upon the bed, the Donna Fioretta playing heartily upon his flute, without however managing to get the instrument to sound even one true note.

"What have we here?" said Ugolotto, his tongue growing almost numb in his mouth as he gazed on the young woman's shape. "Has the good friar already performed services?"

"Indeed he has not!" cried the young woman, looking up. "Though he did do a great deal to guide me along the true path, he found himself unable to proceed after giving the first oblation."

3. "No, I cannot cross," said Madhusudan in a somewhat nasal voice, in calculated tones, "for by my vows I am not able to touch either dew or mist, snow or ice, water of marshes or that which pours from above,—and in particular I am not allowed to touch water like this, which flows across the earth in such a torrent. No indeed, I cannot commit violence to water bodies or approve of such deeds when committed by others!"

The two men, Madhusudan and Vishvatma, stood before the roadway which, due to the seasonal rains, had overnight become a veritable river of muddy-brown water, carrying with it broken sticks; swirling, its current bearing palm fronds and the shield-like leaves of aquatic, nymphaceous plants dragged from some near-distant pond. The sky overhead was grey; the houses of the village were for the most part humble, though some did show signs of modest luxury. In the distance, across the way, out of the growth of banyan and densely-leaved jamun trees, rose the dark spire of the temple where she, the Green-Complexioned Adho-Mukhi, carved out of fig wood, bejeweled and dressed in costly vestments, stood, was to be worshipped.

Vishvatma was short, moon-faced, thick-lashed, his body tending toward the chubby. He wore a loose white robe. Madhusudan was tall and lean, with hollow cheeks and mournful dark eyes. He was completely naked except for a loin-cloth, and a mouth-cover in order to keep him from accidentally swallowing beings born of air or smoke.

So, the two holy men stood before the road which seasonal rains had turned into a muddy river, each wanting to get to the other side so as to perform their daily devotions to the Green-Complexioned Adho-Mukhi. A cowherd came, inclined his head respectfully toward the duo, then waded through the water, leading two heavy-uddered cows. Then came others—a thatch cutter bearing his bundle and blade; a porter, balancing a basket of rice on his head; a pair of fishermen, talking boisterously, their beards overgrown and nets tucked under their arms.

"Well," said Vishvatma with a shrug of his shoulders, "it looks like I will also have to venture into the wet. I have already missed my morning visit to the temple, and dare not stay away any more."

"Do as you desire. I, however, will not follow, for surely I would feel regret, like Indra fallen from heaven."

"If you wish, get on my back and I will carry you," said Vishvatma.

"Indeed not," replied Madhusudan with a sneer beneath his mouth cover. "As I have already emphatically said, I will not be party to violence toward water bodies—whether directly or indi——"

Madhusudan cut short his words, for his ears had suddenly been assaulted by the sound of rustling cloth, of thighs moving with delicate seduction—a sound to him more dangerous than the roar of a lion or the hiss of a poisonous serpent. He looked. A woman stood by their side, a woman redolent of perfume, her face powdered with lotus pollen, whose costume and every gesture spoke of her profession.

The woman, seeing the way blocked by water, pouted and stamped one of her pretty lac-dyed feet on the ground—for to cross would surely be detrimental to her costume, to that finery which was one of the main tools of her livelihood.

Seeing this female human being, this creature in such close proximity, Madhusudan recoiled, as if from some blazing fire or the edge of some hazardous precipice. Vishvatma, on the other hand, smiled, quite innocently. He saw that the woman was in distress.

"I am about to venture across," he said, "and if you wish, I would be quite willing to carry you on my back."

The woman's face brightened; she giggled. "Normally I would not dare put a holy man to such trouble," she said. "But in such circumstances as these . . ." And without finishing her sentence, she climbed, somewhat awkwardly it must be said, onto Vishvatma's back.

Madhusudan watched in dumbfounded amazement as the two made their way through the water, as Vishvatma cheerfully deposited his burden on the other side, afterwards waving back to his colleague.

Madhusudan made no gesture of recognition. In disgust he turned and paced evenly away, with due caution, carefully avoiding greenery and life, avoiding living particles of clay or cow dung, and murmuring to himself, "I must stay away from a woman even if she is a hundred years old and missing her nose and ears—how much more so one richly dressed and bred to inspire lust! Indeed, Vishvatma commits a great sin by lending assistance to such a creature, whose sound, shape and smell will surely cause his downfall, will destroy his merit as fire destroys wood. In the future I doubt not that he will roam through myriad cycles of inferior births."

4. Relics were manufactured wholesale from the bones of dogs and pigs and sold for healthy profits, but looking at the monks you would think they were the poorest of the poor, for they went about in modest clothing and ate sparingly of food in public, saving their appetites for once they were safe in the monastery, when they could drink and eat as much as they liked, now and again kissing their comrades on the lips.

GESTURE OF BOWING

1. There was an immortal named Chiao Ch'i who lived in Yinfang. Before going to the market, he would rub a special kind of mercury on his cash. He bought whatever he wanted and returned home. A few hours later the cash would come floating back to him.

2. A boy, who lived in a small village near Malampur Lake, did not have any clothes, so instead wore eight serpents. Wherever he went, people avoided him. As he grew older, his body began to take on the appearance of wet clay. He killed a number of demons in the area and used their skulls to drink wine from, but still no one would talk with him.

3. Ugolotto, overjoyed at this opportunity, lost no time in informing Donna Fioretta that, though he was but a lowly toad, no one knew better the mysteries of the second coming. She, excited beyond bounds at the prospect of further enjoyment, begged him to do with her

as he wished. The young man, needing not to be asked twice for a service he was passionate to render, threw off his garments and proceeded to take his pleasure, showing Fioretta that, though he was not the least attractive in face or body, he could make her pray to heaven as well as any priest in the land, his shepherd's crook being as firm as the crosier of a bishop.

The sun was already shining its light through the windows when Fra Bernardo awoke. He leaped from the bed, rubbed the small of his back, which was quite sore, and blinked his itchy eyes. Ugolotto was near at hand, whistling a sprightly tune while tidying the chamber from the previous night's activity.

"Ugolotto," the friar cried, "it is already late in the morning! I have services to attend! Why did you not awake me?"

Ugolotto grinned. "My dear Fra Bernardo," he said good-humoredly, sticking out his belly, "the cock crowed eight times before the matins bell tolled, and since that did not awake you I could not guess what would!"

MANY-COLORED EYEBROWS

1. Fish can't be drowned, ashes can't be burnt. Completely used up, no one can use you.

2. Harmony is overrated.

3. Irene had her son's eyes gouged out, plunging the city into seventeen days of darkness, in which giant bats swam through the air.

4. Originally, everything in the universe was yellow. That is why this color is the most frightening.

5. If you're lucky, you'll end up like some choliambic poet.

6. When she woke up, she discovered that her eyebrow box was missing. Did it change her ability to see?

7. The tree was already half dried up. Hadn't been

watered. For years. Put the hose under it. Fungus growing on it. No fruit one green branch a harpsichord of fifty-two strings when played phoenixes would fly down.

8. Things were composed standing in crowds the stench of subways some lonely bum pushing his way soaked in his own piss has the car all to himself.

9. For her thighs, she used a smegma made from: leaves of the castor oil plant, croton, peeled and dried narcissus bulbs.

10. To get rid of wrinkles, she mixed in her bathwater a substance made from: euphorbia grease, bryony roots, orobino flour, the head of a burnt squid, and honey.

11. Traffic has a swirling sound. For future generations, let this be noted.

ENTITIES

1. The glass was now empty. The trail, a thin, squiggly line, ran from it, across the floor, disappearing behind the bookshelves.

He did not stop to reason, but, as he went along, unsavory, disjointed thoughts came to him of their own accord and he grew alarmed. The full consequences of that pinkish-yellow trail did not however occur to him until he saw the creature's head peep out from behind the *Complete Writings* of Blake. At first he did not register the lidless eyes, tiny and dull, or the wormlike elongation to which they were attached. Then, as he witnessed the vibrating, agile way it twisted out and glided over his knee, he became filled with disgust.

With great speed it slithered across the room, leaving a thin pinkish-yellow trail behind it. When it reached the opposite wall, it rose up, as if trying to climb the vertical surface. Realizing the impossibility of the task, it drew its body together, turned and reared its repellent head some bright moon of sour bliss. The tiny, dull eyes seemed to search about the room. With a smooth, watery motion it lay its forepart down lengthwise beside the rest of its body.

What disturbed Louis most about the creature was not its appearance, as appalling as it was, but the incredibly nimble way it moved, which left the impression that it was endowed with some form of predatory intelligence. His primary impulse was to destroy it.

He picked up the *Webster's Unabridged Dictionary*, which lay near at hand. It was by far the heaviest volume he owned.

With bare feet he slowly and quietly advanced. When he was quite near, less than two feet away, he raised the dictionary over his head. His arms trembled. He stretched them out so the dictionary was poised over the creature, which made a sudden, unexpected, rippling movement with its body. He let the book drop, at the same moment shutting his eyes.

He stood rigid for a brief period and then opened them, just in time to see the last whipping, spasmodic movements of the thin, boneless body. The head and forepart of the thing lay crushed under the heavy volume.

2. Jacques de Plomb loved to hear the sound of his own voice. So did others. A thousand pines stood and listened.

3. In India there is a man who dines on nothing but nails. He has a clear complexion and is rather thin. In the

same country there is another man who never eats food or drinks water.

4. When Bernasconi was told to hold his tongue he took it wildly in his arms and kissed it with liberal passion.

5. Happy things:
    A statue with grass growing high around it.
    Water when it boils.
    Marmots.
    A man who travels a long way and is greeted by friends.

MALADJUSTMENT

1. The weather, a humid essence perforated by a soft and pleasant light, played its role on their state of mind. The low country let out a fecund odor, and seeds, of dandelions and other plants, drifted languidly through the heavy air.

The sound came through the brush and moved across the trail. Hooves beat over the earth. The horses, somewhat agitated by the weather, snorted and swatted their backsides with tails, a reflex meant to drive away stray bugs which tended to adhere there.

"They're restless," said the aunt with her dull carnation lips. They were the only thing visible beneath the shade of her hat. "I'm so glad that I have the choice to dress cool or warm, as the weather tells me. I would be dying if this blouse wasn't so light."

The man riding beside her listened and smiled.

Kendra silently took up the rear. The massive round of horseflesh quivered beneath her. Summer, a tepid jelly. Surrounding the girl's maturing spirit and tying it to raw and potent nature.

Later, the trio dismounted by a brook. A picnic was produced and they ate and the horses ate grass and drank water. The aunt and her man-friend talked in low, smooth voices. Kendra finished her refreshment quickly, and wandered into a field, where she picked flowers and lived within herself. Upon looking around, and returning, she found her companions gone. Their laughter could be heard as it disappeared, off into the trees and bushes beyond. The steeds remained. The brown and glistening coat, of the one whom she had been atop, a small blotch of white marking its forehead.

And there were thoughts, actions, touches that never die. Her heredity, like his, was good. As the Countess of Pembroke, profligate instincts swelling, from her vidette. Or Lucrezia, and her father, the stiff Pope Alexander VI, *cum magno risu et delectatione.*

2. Where was he who invented curtains reincarnated?

3. The proprietor stood at the door of the Café Florence aggressively smoking a filtered cigarette in the weak glow of the early afternoon sun. She walked by, along the sidewalk of Columbus Street, gobs of black filth, decades old, clinging to the grey surface.

"Good morning, Miss," he said, his mouth opening in a watery grin, the muscle inside flopping out.

With a comment not quite saucy enough for his taste, she proceeded on her way, crossing before traffic, and entering at the side door of Big Al's, the light of day extinguished behind that closing rectangle of steel. The faces, atop squat figures, which squirmed in chairs, or sometimes sat immobile, eyes dull, minds lapping at this blatant show of degeneration. The matinée.

As some, noble born, are attracted to the stable boy for the very odor that lingers around him, as if it were new mown hay, oil of rose, or scent of jasmine. Those bright days, when tourists from the richest cul-de-sacs of Asia, businessmen transported from Europe, politicians, countenances chiseled and cold, each, in their own telltale manner, lounged their way in. But this was before. The traditions intimated by Apuleius discarded; the sacred goat of Mendes of which Herodotus spoke looked upon as a sin of ages and races past.

4. Annoying things:
People who never pay for drinks.
People who talk loudly outside their houses.
The sound of a clock.
The sound of someone turning the pages of a newspaper.
Too many quickly moving legs.

5. So in her early middle age she sat, on the porch of the house, a relatively grand structure, bought with family riches, yet a far cry from the pedestal of her former days of glory. Exquisite reminiscences. The eyes of Kendra Roberts wandered over the green lawn, scanned the tops of the quivering trees, into the pale blue sky where she could see the past some sphalerite canter tied down in a cocoon of that great Clydesdale.

6. Rex Brown would stretch out his right hand and five digits would appear, five menhirs, lingams, one bound with marital ring, representing the fecundation of an equal singularity of yoni, some paranymphal ensō with a standard atomic weight of 196.966569(4). The collar of his shirt encompassed a head of no large magnitude, spectacles bestraddling the nose, thick lenses covering the eyes, the sun, the moon. A willowy form wandered about the room, gliding upon the epicenter of the universe, that place where an undefined commodity was formed.

"What is the project at hand?" he wondered.

His last show had been delineated along the lines of *Spruce and Elm Twig*, a sublime conception telling of the reductions and refinements of our leafy friends, the voyeuristic and arcane elements of their branches, as well as the hydroconscious implications of their roots. Needless to say, his effort was well appreciated by the educated masses, for their frontal lobes are indeed slavering for stimulation.

Now here he was, a being of multi-cosmic dimensions, the rapid exchange of electrical impulses jetting through his prosencephalon cells to congeal into an idea, a notion, something for the world at small to sigh, gasp and grunt about. Across the fertile fields of his mind frolicked visions, beatific scenes—slender tigers of the tropical jungles of intellection unveiled themselves to his misted hub of creativity. Flatness held the ultimate depth. The Devonian period had lasted a mere sixty million years. There was an intricate architecture to a straight line. Nature in fact was a mere imitation of art, a female ichneumon depositing her eggs in an atom bomb of absurdity.

7. He had lived his life creating—creating his own environment—and developing—a supra-keen sense of aesthetics. Believing in: advancement, culture propelled forward, not through social or political movements (they all in the end made men turn murderer or coward, and even the most promising were perverted, tainted by the stench of power) but through refinement of taste, the appreciation of delicate sensation.

8. The night of the vernissage arrived. A long-anticipated event. Affluent women with steel for eyes fondled broad checkbooks which were in fact the reincarnations of people who in previous lives had mistreated inanimate objects. Young men in shimmering shirts chatted quietly, their stances decidedly hip-shot. A tall blonde cackled into her wine, a few low men orbiting her heavenly body. A grave-looking gentleman strode the room, the perfume of Wall Street lingering about his person. A dubious individual in a second-hand dinner jacket meekly slid from group to group, listening with attentive ears.

"Where is his new work?" whispered a small and eager woman to a man of journalistic appearance.

"Why, I couldn't say," was the reply. "The rooms are quite empty. I can only guess that there will be some kind of an unveiling in the course of the evening."

"It will be marvelous. You know, I bought a *Twig* from his last show."

"You're one of the lucky ones. His work is quite precious."

"Ah, there he is now though! There's Brown coming in the door just now!"

Indeed, Rex had slipped into the place, his limbs jerking like those of a marionette inside his oddly-fitting clothes. Several glasses of gallery wine were necessarily partaken of before he could be made to speak in a semicoherent fashion.

"Your work?" inquired a few voices evasively.

"Best yet," said Rex, a few drops of wine running down his thrice-shaven pale chin.

"Yes. . . . But. . . . Well. . . . Could you explain it?" came a tremulous whisper which sounded like a number of promethea moths fluttering about.

"Rather subtle," said Rex, taking in the expanse of the room with a gesture.

"Most subtle."

"Fine."

"Deep!"

"Profound!" shouted a man with an indefinite European accent.

Murmurs grew to waves of vocal enthusiasm, splashing about the place, running in and out of ears, reverberating, as sound in seashells, and turning dull life into reciprocal emotions of heartfelt, cultural glory.

"But what next?" was the common sentiment. "What more can he do beyond this? How can he go beyond such ultimately fine draftsmanship, such conceptual grandeur, such homogeneity of surface and substance?"

Rex Brown shrugged his shoulders and filled his glass with purple magic, taking a sip, a draught, his lips sinking foremost, to the depth of his cranium, crawling complete into the aforementioned glass, feet clattering at the rim, dissolving or disappearing into fine fumes of cheap burgundy.

"It's quite empty," said a human creature pointing at the receptacle.

"Ah!" was the general reply. "But not as empty as he was!"

9. Mr. Toho, obedient to the ways of nature, would only copulate in spring, when the peach trees were in blossom. Poor Mrs. Toho! Desperately she waits for the petals to fall.

10. A long time ago there was a woman who found out that her husband was a ghost. All her relatives and neighbors begged her to call in an exorcist, but she refused.

"Love is difficult to come by in this world," she said. "Why should I care about my husband's pedigree?"

NOTHING TO HIDE

1. It was a cool October night, vulvic darkness enveloped the world, black, inky as wet soot. The atmosphere was still, cracked by the howl of the dog, shattered; scraping leaves. A first frost salted the wounds of the earth. Houses slept, anesthetizing humans between the membranes of clean sheets, fleshy duvets. Only the regular prick of the clock. The foul snore, some primitive fin, indicative of life.

A bench sat in the gloom, as if on a pitiful tragicomic stage, its white, wrought-iron frame illumining a vague form. Sagging over and dripping. Silent and sealed. Investing the air around it with a dull sorrow. No breath batted its lips, and from its head a faint trickle of blood still ran to the ground.

2. A cloud floated across the sky. A group of birds, hungry, came along and ate it.

Can you imagine them flying about? Rain dripping from their wings.

3. Happy man's method for turning into grass:
Dine every day on antelope horns. Walk in windy places. Make friends with the Poplar clan. Sit quietly with fingers spread out.

4. In the white-walled sitting room of a hospital a man waits. Nurses shuffle by. The receptionist and a doctor make small talk. He can hear them giggle. The soda machine hums. He is doing like his father did: Waiting.

The late hours of the night are forced in. He uses the restroom. The toilet stalls are immaculate. Everything is aseptic, covered in a pure whiteness, the mysterious sheen of life and death, an uncertain halo clouding theories of transmigration and achromatizing faith in the Body and Blood of Christ. He washes his hands, dries them, and washes them again. He paces the floor nervously. So this is what it is to be a man, to feel the results of sensual propulsion and have one's spirits crushed under the joy of responsibility, only trying to do the right thing, pawing the ground, a calf turned bull, snorting under the strain of an expanding belly and a shrinking imagination.

A nurse quietly calls him in. He cannot make out her words. He nods. A boy! A baby boy, with transparent skin, wrinkled and ugly, yet a breathing creature to be sure. Its eyes sleepily contort as they are confronted by the melting appearance of its parents' smiling faces. A mixture of tenderness and repugnance overcomes the father. The mother holds the child to her breasts, a glow of satisfaction on her face.

SLOW AMULETS

1. Absinthe spilled on the lawn.

2. Electric lights defining space.

3. Wind licking the leaves, broken whisky bottles on the bank, their necks full of dirt. He, who had sprouted from those folds of flesh, the animal exit, would cast his line into the water and enjoy the hollow sound of the sinker as it disturbed a black pond, a bird crying from a naked branch.

At school he would fumble at his desk, clumsily manipulating a chewed-up pencil. The classroom cool, the door far away, and further away: the houses. A road wound into the green hills, the hunting ground. His mother insisted on him wearing a wool sweater; itching. The grass, heady, tempting, caressed his nose. He played football with the neighborhood boys. In the living room, evening, spread out on his stomach. Their couch was a vivid peridot and the wallpaper had pink flowers, the passé décor of a lower middle-class home. He spent time lying on the blue rug, staring at the ceiling in cataleptic reveries, finding witches on brooms and big-nosed heads, nightmares amidst the texture of the plaster you jellyfish monster of radial symmetry.

Guitar lessons. A dead uncle. Missed classes. A boy stole his jacket. A crush. She was thin, insignificant, ignored him, smashed him. Drama, opening up, the free and easy atmosphere, making jokes on stage and becoming familiar with his classmates who were saucer-shaped. The teacher liked him and gave him the lead role in the school play. A girl who sat next to him looked at him shyly, but she was not pretty. He wanted her, but procrastinated. She changed schools. He showed talent. The play was a failure, lines forgotten, a jeering crowd.

Misery—sleeping in a barrack full of repellent young men, their snoring keeping him awake half the night and then being hustled out of bed long before dawn, the air still cold and his head groggy and thick. Showering without privacy, his body under the continual scrutiny of those forced companions, a gang of young men not unlike himself, hopeless cases who found some kind of masochistic solace in scrubbing along with the herd, a circus of larvae.

The rations were intolerable: overcooked roast beef that merely became perforated under the pressure of his knife, the rubbery slices swimming in a pool of brown, watery sauce, bubbles of oil floating on top reflecting rainbow hues like gas station puddles; French fries from the freezer, the reconstituted potato turning mealy under the gums; dead vegetables, greens cooked into a boggy pâté; old white bread that formed a sickly paste in the mouth; canned fruit, bubbling in an unsavory sweet syrup that slid down the throat like preserved baby toes.

Constant flatulence, a weak mind, just barely joined to an overtaxed digestive system. He tried to battle this dietary ruin by importing fresh fruit. He grew thin, porous, light-headed. The forces retreated and gullies ran with blood.

He stayed with his parents. His father began giving him hard eyes over the brim of a morning paper that slobbered banalities about grand jury proceedings and insecurity in the labor force. His mother moped about, sighing. He would go for strolls, half hoping to run into an old acquaintance: some girl he once vaguely knew or a fellow from school. A blind cat walked in front of him. The streets were empty; he longed for the action of the real world, the friction of the city, with all its naughty grooved women, life. The fantasies of the human being.

Walls bare, furnishing ugly: a plaid couch in the living room and a few rickety chairs around a contemptibly cheap table in the kitchen. He would watch from his third-story window as they walked by. They would patrol the street for a half hour or forty-five minutes, slinking back and forth, taking their time at their libidinous perambulations, before some silent old land boat crept up, first passing somewhat beyond them and then coming to a dead halt, like the driver suddenly recognized someone they knew. The woman would feign nonchalance as she approached with quick restrained strides and then peer into the car window. They were driving off, around the corner, no doubt to commit acts of quadrupedal criminality.

   He jogged down the three flights of stairs, his footsteps echoing against the cinder block walls, and arrived on the sidewalk outside, bare and solemn, stretching as far as the eye could see in either direction, intersections apparent in the distance by the blinking of traffic lights. Turning around a corner he recognized one of the frequenters of his neighborhood, walking in front of him, a half-block away. He had only seen her from a distance: wretchedly hovering about, in a costume of heart-wrenching impertinence. He slowed his pace. From the perimeter of night a whistle, a shriek of pain. The woman bolted around, a leaping newt, presuming that he had called. She stood there and waited. He approached, could make out thick, stockinged legs. They rose up, revealing a fine line of white snow—and then disappeared into the shadows, the coupling pen, that he might wish lit by the blast of a cannon.

   Her ringed eyes imposed themselves on him as he drew up, a dismal confidence playing in them. He felt a coarse longing as he met her gaze, but passed on, feeling uneasy and low as he prowled amongst the tall buildings, acrid smoke draining from his watery mouth.

   4. Infatuated with militant subjects, the construction of pipe bombs, how to blow up cars, etc. He listened to the news more closely, formed conspiracy theories and

fantasized about an anarchized America, where every man would live by the strength of his wits and the magnitude of his arsenal. His meager military training served as the seed out of which sprung a bivouacked view of the world, nations contacting like fragile china, ready to splinter apart at the slightest pressure, every man secretly at loggerheads with the next, the minutiae of individuality predestined to ignite, each particle rubbing up against the next until the combined friction would cause a massive conflagration, sending society into a state of brutal, carnivorous warfare.

He bought himself a used rifle and practiced on the edge of town, letting go at green beer bottles and tin cans. The trigger-pulling excited his sense of power; he imagined every slug in a man's heart; every movement of the mechanism a veritable act of coitus.

He felt as if he had a purpose, grinning to himself with thoughts of his secret agenda, making mental blueprints for gross acts of terrorism, forming far-fetched scenarios from which he emerged a hero of a new order, beads of sweat sliding down his powder-blackened face and women clinging to his sinewy arms as he walked over a newly emerging Earth.

He developed a severely nihilistic viewpoint, strongly opposed to fatalism yet perfumed with superstitious fear. He began to avoid the number thirteen and became nervous on dates that numerically coincided, such as the third of March; he thought he could read cautionary signs in the flight patterns of certain birds—the crow, the magpie; how a sparrow pecks.

5. There are beings that look like bolts of lightning. They carry with them nooses, drums, and goads.

6. There is a kind of pearl that if thrown at the sky will break it. A certain Taoist had one of these a long time ago.
He cast it without even much effort, and the sky became like a fractured egg shell.

7. It was on the estate of an old mansion, belonged to an eccentric woman. Weeds grew from the shaded walkways, the untrimmed trees strangled by morning glories formed rococo hedges, psychotic, stray tendrils reaching out, quivering with life, and blossoms opening up from amongst the green mass like the mascaraed eyes of an aged whore. There was an abandoned tennis court, a corpse of luxury, bursting poison, nettles from sharded clay. The cats' graves were lined up under a couple of sycamore trees; little wooden crosses with silly, infantile names scraped in, grain-rotten; all those cute little diminutives that certain women hold so dear, those sickly sweet nomenclatures that mince off the tongue with a fricative spring that compact a number of syllables into a space where the ear can hardly tolerate one. There were fifty or sixty of these crosses. That woman had grown lonely in her old age and formed a monomania for feline companionship. A shame, the so-called noble sentiments, wasted in their fragile years on the cat deity, that heartless creature that proudly sucks up emotivity. If overfed, their bellies sag; if undernourished, they look sickly and

pitiful. Never do you see them with the sinewy muscles of the leopard or the smooth gait of the panther, claws tensed to kill-darkened earth.

But:

There was a crude glass pavilion in the middle of the property where he would sit. The windows were streaked with dirt and gave the daylight morbid tints; at night the place glowed, moonlight stabbing in. In the day he would bring a book, at night liquor, the essence of agave azul, steeped in nocturnal loneliness, his brain unreeling with the tequila, the sweetness of blood, as it floated through silent tangents, building dream towers and then burning them down in mental paroxysms of temulent rage.

The very incense of liquor acted as a catalyst, setting off obscure hues, bringing out base colors and highlighting them like an over-varnished painting; stiffening certain flaws of his organism, showing where his patina had been botched, making a mad science of the copulation that had brought him to life, adding a beaker of spice to make the brew froth.

8. Underground, the world condensed into a sort of rathole, crawling through a strange abbatial maze, always trying to move higher, in an instinctive attempt to reach broad day, in a longing for vegetation. But no matter what the effort, he was continually backsliding, always falling deeper toward an abyss: a great cavernous hole with a treacherous arrow pointing down. He could make out a vague, capricious staircase leading up to a spot of blue, a sign of gratification barely discernible, a veiled luster

receding in the distance like a mirage, a phantom. An aqueous blackness swelled up around him, a dreary slime. He felt himself jailed in his own mind, doomed to wander endlessly in the cascading rebus of dreamland, all things being mere representations, nothing clearly defined.

The dress was soiled with a splash of mud.

A gap; a fragment missing from a manuscript: Ladders. Steps. Distensions. Everything turned feverish, a putrescence-coated dungeon. The smell of an abattoir; miasma.

Panic, fear. He pounded and kicked at the pillars of his conception, desperate for release. The phasma trembled, convulsed, everything shivering like an undressed child in the snow.

9. Walking in the town of Q——, around the old gun factory, crawl through a hedge and find yourself in the local cemetery. First you fall in the way of the older section; hiking up a little incline you are greeted by a rebar archway wrapped in white roses, melancholy flowers, petals slightly yellowed like an old ivory comb that has seen some woman's flaxen hair grey. Pensive maidens stand frozen atop pillars and sit sadly on tombs, lichen growing in the folds of their petrified garments, giving them the tonality of a mezzotint. Family plots covered with wood chips, or fading, patchy grass; some have merely a cold concrete slab to conceal the decomposed remains of a once prospering line. Morbid decorations are there, carrying a mood of intricate horror, like certain woodcuts of Dürer or Brueghel; you see: stone urns and

penetrating obelisks, faded tombstones with decorative writing, and horseshoe ones indicative of dual graves, bonding couples together even as they rot, as the emptied cage mildews, turns to dust. Some are cracked or broken under piles of pine needles or half buried beneath mossy earth; of some just the base is left, a stub, all identification having disappeared. A statuary baby, worn and hostile, crouches on this memorandum of life: 1 year, 5 months, 21 days. Military graves stating rank and regiment, a limp flag shedding its dirt-stained colors to the glory machine. The small Muslim section: nero antico tombstones bearing the hieratic writing of an Indo-Iranian language, some of them with a rose chiseled in the corner. The sepulchers, buried in a hillside, thin flutes, chimney-like pipes, air vents, peeping through the ground up top. Others stand in the open, with columns, peripteral, the glass doors behind iron grating. Looking in one sees the white engraved walls marking tombs, a stone fruit bowl on a pedestal sits in the middle of the marble floor, an offering to the shades.

As you approach the newer section of the cemetery, you see fewer and fewer standing stones, until there are none. Rows of symmetrical graves sink in the earth, many bearing Masonic symbols and all are close together, economic. Occasional ganglia of flowers left by caring, guilty relatives—they colorfully spurt up, adding flashes of contour to frightening regularity. Angry crows scream. We look down: one headstone, much like the rest, brass submerged in marble, a little wreath molded in the center, a scroll bearing the deceased's name, date of birth, and death, in the corner.

IRREVERSIBILITY

1. Outside the moon is a shutting eye some great confusion of stillness anxiety of the void or some parting fulfillment ripping away the darkness from that thing beating on a big red drum high tide of autumn.

2. Things that come in threads:
    Time.
    Truth.
    Wine.

3. Method for preparing cinnabar sauce:
Procure half a pound of cinnabar, two pounds of lead, two ounces of mercury, four ounces of Szechuan lovage, three duck eggs, lubricating oil. Melt the lead in an iron vessel and add the mercury. A skin will form at the top of the vessel. Peel this off and let it cool and pound it in a mortar with the Szechuan lovage. When a paste is formed, move the formula to a copper vessel and add the duck eggs. In another mortar grind the cinnabar.

Dribble the lubricating oil in the copper vessel mixture while adding the cinnabar.

4. I had just left the public library and stood on Fifth Avenue, before the torrent of traffic; a rush of imbecility—the daily pilgrimage of the bedlamites. The language of Crébillon fils, which I had been perusing, filled my mind, and I equated the bipeds frisking around me with the images penned by that improper French author, a man today little known, less read, a bit better than Voltaire and, in my estimation, equal to Diderot.

The depression caused by the loss of my lobster, earlier that summer, found relief in scrutinizing the works of unread authors. It had cut its way through its leash while I was walking it through Central Park. I had been watching the toy sailing boats on the lake, and when I looked around, my shellfish was gone.

The library's hours were limited. At five o'clock I found myself shunted onto the street, to join the round of pedestrians, be brushed against by their gold-rushing legs.

The mist of fantasy broke before me as the nerves in my hand ascertained a grasp, the contact of damp human epidermal tissue. The proprietor of those five moist caecilians turned out to be a man I had not seen in a number of years, grim of visage, acne-scarred, hair tending toward the oily, generously salted with dandruff, a nose well peppered, dirty secretions plugging the ducts of the skin.

"Carlos," he said, something probably intended as a

smile wriggling across his face. "Long time no see. The physical body rots away: what is the hard and fast body of reality?"

"The mountain flowers bloom like brocade, the valley streams are brimming blue as indigo," I replied blandly.

It was Barry Lagerlof, a fellow I knew from my stint at Peach-flower Monastery in Petrolia a few years earlier. He was likable enough I suppose, under his blemished exterior. But he had an annoying habit of jointly quoting, and instigating, the koans of the Zen masters of old, a trick he seemed to have unfortunately retained from his days as a Buddhist acolyte.

"Nice to run into you like this Lagerlof," I said. "It's so easy to lose touch with one's . . . friends . . . in a big city. And how are you? What do you do these days?"

"Better than ever, Carlos," putting his hand humidly on my shoulder. "I have inherited the family business— the Kosher pizzeria chain. Big stuff with the Hasidim. No more bumming around town, wasting time at the library. And you? What's your current line of work? Not still chasing rainbows, I'm sure."

"No," I lied, with what I presume to have been a bright look, "I am editor-in-chief of a publication, both ambitious and new, targeting young immoral consumers."

"Praise be to Mi Hu," he replied with a chuckle. "I was afraid you were still dedicating yourself to those dirty old French books."

"Oh, no," I said suavely. "For that sort of entertainment I visit the night clubs. I buy drinks which the bartenders don't know how to make, ask various young women questions they don't quite understand, and receive replies I don't quite want to hear. And do you," I continued, "—Do you go out . . . enjoy the night life?"

"The sacred tortoise drag its tail? Certainly not! Not really, at least. Maybe an occasional concert, a play possibly. Or the opera; *we* might do that. We . . . I just got married you know. Yes, no need to look so amused. I tied the knot."

I have to say that I was not merely amused, but absolutely stunned. I had always considered Lagerlof to be the type who would never get married—a condemned bachelor. Aside from his physical ensemble, which did not seem to me capable of inspiring a woman with any sort of overmastering desire, there was that obnoxious habit of his, those koans, the way he would stab at your ears with them mercilessly. He was a coarse man.

"She tripped over my foot in one of my venues," he explained. "That's how we met. She bruised her knee. It was beautiful—her knee I mean. I told her that I didn't like to play games—I could support a wife—I needed a spiritual woman, a life companion. If you don't grab it when you see it, you'll be thinking about it when you're a thousand miles away. I am the happiest man in the world—I'm in love, Carlos!"

"She must be a . . . special lady," I faltered. "I . . . I'm curious to see her—to meet her."

"Well of course, Carlos, of course. You'll come to dinner—reed flowers drenched in moonlight—I'll show her off to you. Tomorrow? At six-thirty?"

Barry scribbled his home address on the back of a business card. With a wave of his clammy hand he thrust his body into the back seat of a yellow cab and joined the rush hour traffic.

As I walked over to Sixth Avenue, to catch the F train, matrimonial visions asserted themselves throughout my cerebral hemisphere. I recalled Balzac's *Marriage Contract*, ending with the desperate husband speeding away on an India-bound ship, his avaricious wife, mother-in-law, and all hopes of happiness laughing mockingly behind him. But that was mere romance. In the real world surely every creature with half an upper lip can find an amorous-minded companion.

I was still wondering about this as I sat in the Little Morocco Bar on Grove Street, puffing languidly on a hookah and enjoying a Pall Mall cocktail. The despondency I had been wallowing in removed itself from the forefront of my concern. The lobster had escaped. I had probably been too lax with the leash. There was still a life to be led and queer fish like Barry to figure, to marvel at.

I must say that it interested me. Running across old acquaintances often strums strange chords. The Lagerlof episode had made me thirsty. It added piquancy to the first Pall Mall, so I suffered a second.

My curiosity had not diminished as I crawled along the Long Island Expressway the next evening, in the rusted and rattling Peugeot borrowed from my uncle Eduard. Barry lived in Lake Success and I could feel the grin expand my facial features as I took note of the ostentatious new homes built up along his street—homes that certainly cost money, but just as certainly lacked all but the pretences of good taste.

The new Mrs. Lagerlof answered the door and invited me in. She seemed quite nervous. I was not there to judge her, but merely observe. Actually, I barely caught sight of her face. It seemed that the rear view was quickly given precedence. Conventional clothing, such as can be purchased at just about any parade of shops, though not absolutely devoid of charm, certainly lacking originality—the costume of a billion other women, from the lanes of Taipei to the alleys of Poza Rica de Hidalgo.

So I was ushered into the living room. Barry rose, a glass of white wine wedged between the tips of his thick fingers.

"You've met my sweetheart I see." (His obvious pride I found embarrassing.) "Come on—with your throat, mouth and lips shut, how can you speak?"

"Yes. You two make a beautiful couple," I again lied. Now that I saw her face I felt that I had seen it before. Either that, or I was experiencing déjà vu.

I requested a few fingers of bourbon. My nerves were out of tune and I had high hopes a drink would compose those springy, subtle things. Unfortunately his tongue continued to drum and drift along on its own current.

We sat through twenty-five minutes of monotonous conversation, or really monologue. Lagerlof talked only of himself, his petty ambitions, his annals and talents. His wife did not speak at all, but merely nodded her head with strained familiarity. I tried desperately to make a few easy and witty remarks, but the words that tripped from my teeth were absurd, stiff and pedantic. The three of us looked at each other in astonishment—I sensed that the planets must have been in some slight disarray that evening.

Fortunately, dinner was served. I cannot say that I recommend the table of Lagerlof, but then again there are few tables, either public or private, that I would recommend with any sense of honesty. It was a mildly bland seafood supper: razorback clams, a few snails, a loaf of bread, a bottle of recent wine.

As I politely attempted to clear my plate of its contents my suspicions increased. I felt an absolute certainty as to a previous knowledge of the good hostess. Indeed, I had spent some rather intimate hours with the persona in question. From those insolent eyes and clipped gestures I could tell I was not mistaken.

After the salty course, Lagerlof excused himself to the restroom. His wife retired to the kitchen, to get coffee and dessert. I wiped my lips, folded my napkin with supreme care, and followed her. As I came in she turned toward me in surprise.

"The game's up," I said, grabbing her nose. It came off with little resistance. The creature before me screamed like a baby—as they say her kind do when submerged in boiling water. Her antennae quivered and then swept the air with petulant gestures. Her eyes glistened nervously at the ends of their stalks.

"Please remove yourself from those jeans," I said, calmly and with great dignity. "*You* are going home with *me*."

Unfortunately she was prone to be rebellious and snapped at me.

"You spineless beast," I reprimanded. "Do you know how ridiculous you look in that get-up? It's shameful."

I was not particularly in the mood for a drawn-out scene. I collared her. Sensing the uselessness of further deception, she molted her garments. I grabbed her by an antenna and led her out of the kitchen and toward the front door.

Lagerlof was just then reappearing. He looked shocked, scandalized.

"What are you doing with my wife?" he cried, grabbing at one of the tremulous, red claws. "The valley's single plum flower!"

"Hands off," I parried. "The creature was my lobster before she was your wife. I am in a position of precedence."

"I had no idea though," he stammered. "But I really don't see the difference."

"Then I feel profoundly sorry for you Lagerlof," I said, heading out the door, the creature secure in my grasp. "Women are generally more appealing spouses than shellfish. After all, it's hardly kosher."

"But we have matching temperaments!" he wept. "What will I do with myself?"

"On the left horn of the snail is a kingdom called Resignation. Travel those myriad miles," I advised as I shoved my squirming burden into the passenger seat of the car.

EMERGING FROM A TRANCE

1. The sunflower was large, tall, and around it the girls danced, calling it a wizard. A beam of light shot upward, thirty feet, and down rained blood.
That evening no one looked at the sunset.

2. The remains of the meal littered the table; crumbs of cornbread on the plates, the bones of chicken, the oily, swamp-green deposit of collards cooked with fatback. She, her face tired, hair, touched with grey, somewhat unkempt, its beauty repressed, as was her smile, which was turned upside down. The frying of chicken, the keeping the cabin clean, and quiet—for him, his poetry, and whims.

"Make the coffee strong," he said, to her bent figure, as it went toward the kitchen.

Yes, he has work to do, she thought—work of the mind. Of the vaquero-joint-poet-joint-hunter, philosopher—high-caliber mind.

In the trash were the bones of fowl, so recently

chewed—and she tied the bag, and took it out back to the stable, where the stench would not be known.

His shouts, that night, could be heard all through the valley, as well as the yelps of the dog as it cowered. Paper, tins. Scattered refuse. Flesh-stripped bones. And the stick was raised, fell (on a body of soft fur); boot maneuvering, unreasoned, oblique, screwing, violently, to the surface.

When he came in, her eyes were closed; she feigned sleep. From somewhat distant bushes the dog, still feeling pain, saw the lights expire in the house that rested in the valley, surrounded by high blue-black hills. So white turned to dark, and that to red; and the whimperings—they were heard.

"Leave me alone," he mumbled. "Go back to bed."

The nerve of woman. Or hovering over him. Or shadow, and cold——

"What? . . . Are you crazy?"

But the hands that grabbed were in a mood of certainty, them smooth and rigid as hardest stone. An obvious aberration, as they more dragged than led him out of the room. Obscuration. Except for a form that loomed.

His cries muffled and then the cold of night air, his body half naked. A man (like molten grub), exposed, fat body bound in mere boxers. And the rough ground under his hurried feet. And the sticks batting against his shins. Scratches of brambles. Thrust through the creek. Only the sound of his own heavy breath, damning, and the other's footfall, steady and definite.

Through the tall pines they went, and then down, the aspens drips of white. The half-world; and his captor: noble, erect; horns and plumes forming a foreground against the dark blue sky: smeared with clouds and punctured by moon. Down in the forest's clearing, where he again opened his eyes, the mound of flames licked, and the face was known. That one standing against a backdrop of masks . . . or faces of beasts.

His presence, an emblem, bare body of man, brought forth the sounds; the woodnotes, ululations, snorts, howls, and screeches. So many mouths open in scorn; baring of teeth; blazing and blinking of eyes.

The world was reduced. To the glow of a single flame. A patch in the woods. A blotch of quivering fear.

"Damn you all!" he cried, struggling to his feet, wishing his finger were clenching a trigger.

The black eyes of the *Procyon lotor*; then weasel; otter, skunk, and badger. Odd-toed ungulates. Equids; the horse and ass; and that wapiti (a red hole still showing beneath magnificent antlers) pawing the ground—bugling—a high pitched whistling sound.

Unmanned, he would gladly have retreated, sought refuge in the woods—loped toward his own warm dwelling; but his way was blocked; even the newt licked at his feet as, trembling, he stepped backward, his spine set against a lone tree.

"What—what do you want?" he gasped.

The figure, of genuine power, with the unblinking eyes of a judge, stood before him, an upright stroke before that morose circlet of beasts. The Measurer, that inventor of numbers, holding a reed pen in one hand, a scroll embossed with an eye in the other. *Threskiornis aethiopicus*; the long and downward-curving bill. The tiny head; yet muscular body of man.

"You will be weighed. Your heart."

Anubis. And those teeth of the jackal invited pain to visit the human frame before them.

So—in serrated beads of red. In tortures vicarious and mental. Ape, wearing a disk and crescent, sacred to Thoth and Chensu; dog's head, body simian. Socharis, hawk-headed. Naheb-ka's forked tongue licking at his ears. Serq, her body that of a scorpion, teasing the man's terror with her tail. Each one willing to devour that organ that beat wildly in his chest.

The mole blindly sniffed at him. A moth flitted by his face. Ape stepped forward, bowed before the ibis-headed one, and advanced toward the man. Holding a scale on high, a feather set in one pan.

"We will now weigh your heart against the feather of truth and judgment," were the words which issued from those black, curdled lips, and dripped off that panting tongue.

That hand reached forward, extended. Prehensile fingers touched his breast, and nails incised epidermal tissue, moving to bone.

"I'm alive!" the man screamed, his body, read life, feeling like liquid seeping fast from a broken bag.

The stars were sucked away by the pale morning light, which found her, with face tired and hair touched by grey, kneeling over him, at the foot of that solitary tree.

3. There is a certain river in which stones are found that are actually the bones of a deity who once lived in a nearby mountain. These stones are the color of honey. When these are taken and placed on a pedestal and worshipped, parasols of light will begin to drop from the sky.

4. The streets were crawling with men; the faces of oxen, mules, chipmunks, ferrets; women wriggling like wolfhounds, heads cocking like pheasants, eyes blank as the ostrich. A drizzle of flesh; bellies like pots.

There is a verse that goes with this:

> I chew my bread and cheese—my hunk of onion raw
> Money, glamour
> I crouch and snarl
> Do you think humanity progresses?

During the end of the Dynasty, those in high positions will hurry about, never letting themselves or the people rest.

5. Paul Romuald was reborn as a spoon. Not a demitasse spoon or some sharp-nosed stainless steel fruit spoon, but (as the laws of karma would have it) a rather attractive sterling silver soup spoon, crafted in a Prelude pattern and measuring 6-1/2" in length, with a bowl of 2-1/8" by 1-1/8" and the whole of him weighing in at 37.6 grams (925 parts pure silver, 75 parts alloy).

At first he was rather taken aback by his new body, but, when he saw how much his kind was looked up to by the other items of tableware, he was consoled and accepted his position, if not joyfully, at least with philosophy.

The stream of consciousness is very adaptable.

In his previous life he had taught math, every evening had walked in the park, had been a lonely and sad bachelor/atheist. A man without God or love has little to complain of when he finds himself reincarnated as a piece of fine silverware. There are possibilities much worse, and we can guess that he was aware of this, since foolishness and stupidity are two very different things.

The household where he found himself was decent, and the woman of the house, whose fingers were both slim and warm, polished him frequently enough.

He was thoroughly delighted when the lips of the hostess wrapped themselves around him; he loved very much to feel the base of his bowl press against her warm tongue. He wished he could witness her naked form, and lamented the fact that spoons are not kept more often in the bedroom.

The husband, of course, was another matter. His moustache, as it rubbed against the spoon's silver skin, was very aggravating. Fortunately Paul (we will still call him this) was seldom used by the husband, but frequently by the wife, the latter being much more fond of soups and broths than the former.

Paul realized that he was in love.

Horses gallop, ducks waddle.

He recalled hearing somewhere that women, that

ladies considered 'little things' to be the benchmark of a relationship. And yes, he was little. Not as far as spoons go, of course. He was a giant among spoons. But compared to her, the wife, he was little.

Anyhow, one day she packed a picnic and packed him as well. Not that soup was to be served. We really don't know what her intention was in bringing a soup spoon on a picnic, but she did. Stranger things than this have happened.

Now, the man who went on the picnic with the wife was not her husband. His name was Charles Somayaji. He was born in Naples, Italy, under the name of Carlos Cagliari, and had lived in the Philippines, Germany, and England before moving to Jeu-les-Bois, France, where he changed his name and began studying hatha yoga. He later founded the École Paradigmes Expansion and introduced over nineteen thousand students to yoga, meditation and other mind-body disciplines. He also published a biannual newsletter which had over five thousand subscribers around the world.

A blanket was laid out on the grass, in the shade of a tree. The spoon (Paul) and some forks were removed from the basket, along with food and a bottle of wine. Food was eaten and wine drunk. Charles Somayaji was a vegetarian, but still ate a wing of chicken. He was an abstainer from alcohol, but still drank half the bottle of wine.

He threw his lips onto those of the wife. She fell backward.

In this activity, her foot touched Paul, inadvertently pushing him off the blanket. He felt terribly betrayed.

He lay there on the ground. The day turned to night. The night turned to day. The sun flew overhead. Dusk arrived again. Nights and days came and went in succession. The trees changed their color and buried him in their leaves.

And there he would lie, decaying for the next two thousand five hundred years, before transmigrating to his next life, to be reborn as the god Indra.

6. The spoon family is of very ancient origin, having existed since Paleolithic times.

TREASURES

1. They were arranged in cabinets with exquisite care: a graceful blue-green aqua bottle with twin opposing ear-shaped handles applied at the neck; a green glass amphora flask; a double balsamarium with joined tubular bodies; a translucent cobalt blue rod-formed tubular jar.

He had dreams: of being like the stained glass windows by Perugino in San Salvatore al Monte, or one of Paolo Uccello's in the Duomo of Florence; or something by King Henry VIII's master glazier, Bernard Flower. Glass eyes. Glass fingernails. Tempered glass teeth, able to withstand pressure of twenty-two thousand pounds per square inch.

2. Mr. Korinthian sat down on the patio of the Chez Wanda and ordered his meal. While the waiter was bringing the first course, a dozen delicious oysters, a large tree fell, crushing the life out of that latter and sending the shellfish flying.

"Well, that fellow certainly won't be getting a tip,"

Korinthian said with annoyance, as he watched a cat approach the corpse.

    3. Distracting things:
       Thoughts.
       Flies.
       A woman laughing.
       The smell of mushrooms frying.

    4. Tarchetius, King of the Albans, was not only one of the cruelest, but also one of the most sensual of men. His days he spent devising tortures for his enemies; at night he ate countless dainties, watched his hired flute and harp girls perform and sway their hips lasciviously, and then went forth to have interaction with the most accomplished courtesans in his kingdom.

"*A fronte vel a tergo?*" he asked the prostitute Dexithea on one occasion.

"*A fronte*, by all means," the woman answered with a laugh, "because I am afraid that otherwise you will bite off my braids."

Such was the reputation of the king.

One evening, while he was enjoying a dish of parrots' tongues in aspic and drinking a cup of delicious spiced Lesbian wine, a certain apparition appeared in his apartment, in the form of a great phantom phallus which rose out of the hearth and hung suspended in mid-air, in a most intimidating posture. The king, naturally quite startled, gazed at the object in wonder and then, after somewhat regaining his composure, called for his chief attendant, Faustulus.

"Faustulus," said the king, "either the wine I am drinking is poisoned, and I have gone mad, or a demon has entered my chamber!"

"*Domine*," Faustulus replied, "I do not in the least believe that you have gone mad. If you mean by demon that object which I see suspended in mid-air by the hearth, then it is my duty to relieve your mind, for the thing is nothing more nor less than a phallus of rather grand proportion. Aside from its disembodied state, and its somewhat advanced dimensions, it is in no way different from that which you and I, and all other true men, hold about our persons."

"But it rose up out of the hearth!"

"That, *Domine*, is a mystery."

"What do you suggest I do?"

"I believe the appropriate course on such an occasion would be to send an emissary to the oracle of Tethys, in Tuscany, and ask her opinion of the matter."

"Then by all means depart at once, my dear Faustulus, because it will be impossible for me to abide much in my room while this apparition is here, for I dare not turn my back on it or close my eyes in its presence lest it assault me in a way I am by no means prepared for."

Faustulus, assuring the king that he would make all possible haste, took his leave and within the hour was mounted on a fine horse and riding speedily for Tuscany. Three days later he returned and immediately sought an audience with the king.

"*Domine*," he said, "I have seen the oracle, and she has informed me that the phantom, which in all truth is a manifestation of the god Mars, must be propitiated, in a manner befitting its most singular form. A maiden, a virgin whose matrix has not yet been crossed by man, must have intercourse with it, and the female will thereby bear a son very illustrious for his valor, of surpassing good fortune and strength."

Tarchetius was very relieved upon hearing this news and immediately had his own daughter, Aemilia, sent for, who he trusted was in condition to perform the task, and might thereby bring a noble child into the world to carry on his line.

"Aemilia," he said, "do you see the apparition which hangs there over my hearth?"

"Yes," the young woman replied, her cheeks slightly kindled, "I do see a most strange and, to speak the truth, somewhat intimidating object suspended above your hearth."

"Do not let it frighten you, my dear girl, for I must ask you to act in a manner with it that will require your absolute presence of mind." And the king then went on to instruct her on the task he wished her to perform, not neglecting to give precise details, thinking that she, in her innocence, was altogether ignorant as to the *regulas ludi*.

"Father," Aemilia replied when the king had finished, "due to my love for you and my desire to bear an honorable child that will carry on the line of our most illustrious family, I will sacrifice my modesty to this phantom, though I feel quite certain the action will cause me no little suffering, if not outright agony."

The king, greatly pleased, left the girl alone in his

chamber, himself retiring to another part of the palace to enjoy cheesecakes and the company of his flute girls.

Now Aemilia, though in all appearances the most chaste of maidens, was in fact far from inexperienced in the ways of two-backed beasts. Her appetite for illicit deeds was really far from moderate, and there was no activity she was fonder of than strolling through the stimulating gardens of Venus. Left alone with the phantasm, whose form made her long to know its method of operation, she cast aside her garments and, her young and graceful body fully exposed, approached the object with great eagerness. That apparition however, instead of letting itself be enwrapped in her embrace, withdrew an equal distance to every step she advanced, acting in this way like the proverbial carrot and she the proverbial ass. Much frustrated by this, especially as she was in every way, not only prepared, but almost mad to offer the phantom the pleasures of her body, the young woman sat down on the floor and came apart in tears.

Hearing Aemilia crying, her waiting maid, Roma, an especially modest and beautiful creature, entered the chamber and asked her mistress what was the matter. Aemilia, pointing to the phantom, which still hovered in the air, seeming to mock her with its manner of absolute readiness, explained to the young woman the entire situation.

"But why will the apparition not touch you?" asked Roma.

"Undoubtedly because I am not in that state of virginity in which my father believes me to be, and now, not only am I denied a pleasure which I am truly keen to have, but I risk the anger of the king, who as you know is the most cruel man ever to have issued from woman's womb! For when he sees that the apparition is in no way satiated, but on the contrary seems to have grown rather stouter than otherwise, he will be sure to suspect the truth and punish me accordingly."

"*Domina mea*," said Roma with great composure, "on this account have no fear, for I am your most loyal and devoted servant, and would sooner undergo any rigor, even going so far as to allow this most dangerous-looking phantom to ravage me, than see you suffer in the least. Being completely and in all ways without carnal knowledge, I have every expectation that this strange and rigid phasm will take to me, though in all truth the mere thought of the matter fills me with great fear!"

Aemilia, drying her eyes, assured her servant that there was nothing in the least to be afraid of and that the young lady should be grateful to be able to offer the first fruits of her virginity, not to any ordinary mortal, but to an incarnation of the god Mars, made up of all that was best in the masculine side of the universe without any superfluities.

The handmaid, taking courage from her mistress's words, forthwith undressed and, exposing a body delicate and smooth, laid herself down on the rug in a position calculated to attract the phantom, which in all truth it did, for the apparition immediately altered its angle and proceeded to advance upon the young woman with formidable speed. Roma, in no way defending her gates, but on the contrary inviting the invader to enter, watched with streaming eyes and screams upon her lips as all her citizenry were put to the sword in a most fierce and brutal manner, all her treasures were dragged from their constricted vaults, and, after being doused with quantities of oil, the entire city was put to flame.

Now as it happened, Faustulus, curious in no small degree as to the progress of the campaign which he himself had done so much to forward, entered the chamber, both expecting and hoping to see the phantom in progress with Aemilia. Yet he witnessed nothing of the sort, but instead the handmaid Roma laid out on the rug and at that very moment experiencing the supreme conclusion of passion, while the king's daughter stood by a mere eager onlooker doing her best to *explere libidinem suam effrenatam* by what means she could. Much disturbed at this, he hurried off to inform the king, who, upon hearing the news, cried out with anger and immediately gave orders that both his daughter and her handmaid should be seized for the purpose of putting them to death.

In much need of relaxation after receiving such information and being forced to such an extremity, Tarchetius that evening made his way to the house of the prostitute Dexithea, the most skilled at her profession in the kingdom, carrying with him numerous perfumes to offer the woman as a gift. As it happened, though, the prostitute, having already heard of the king's brutal intention toward the princess and the handmaid, refused all the perfumes, from the aromatic oil of thyme to the sweet extract of lavender, looking at each with very haughty disdain and claiming that she found none of them in the least to her liking. Overcome with concupiscence, not only by the woman's presence, by her body with its soft curves, her rather large hips, her small and pointed breasts, but also by her treatment of him, the king then proceeded to make extract from a certain *radice lenta* which he had in *possessionem suam*, offering the perfume gained thereby to Dexithea by way of last resort.

"You wretch," she said, "I think this smells by far the most putrid of all!"

"Yes," answered the king, "but as the gods are my witnesses, Dexithea, I would have you know that this is made from *glandula vere regium*."

At this she could not help but laugh, and for the first time since the commencement of their interview the king was blessed with a smile. Still, Dexithea was far from pleased with the man's conduct toward his daughter and the handmaid and pleaded their cause, saying that to put the two girls to death was a penalty far outweighing the crime of their petty deception. She then performed for the king *negotium aliquod*, which she knew him to be exceedingly fond of, at every spare breath pleading with her *labia libidines* for the lives of the young women.

The king that evening, in his sleep, further dreamt of Dexithea, coming to him in the form of the goddess Hestia, and telling him on no account to put the princess and her handmaid to death, so that when he awoke, he was convinced that this was an omen and gave orders to suspend the execution. As a milder penalty, he imposed upon the young women the weaving of a certain web in their imprisonment, assuring them that when they had finished the task, they should be given in marriage to respectable men, each according to her own rank.

5. Madhusudan was an ascetic. Aside from the mouth-cover and cloth about his loins, his only possession was a begging bowl. He did not accumulate, or even desire to accumulate, anything—not black salt, ghee or jaggery, that sugar made from the sap of the palm. He would never accept food from a pregnant woman or eat from a vessel contaminated with particles of salt or laterite soil. He never ate the roots of the kamala or stalks of the kumuda, or unripe sugarcane, or half-fried beans or unripe shaddock. When he drank water it always needed to be first thrice-boiled. His face was eternally grave; he never smiled or even smirked and considered laughter a serious sin, the roving comedians and musicians who passed through the village veritable devils.

He spent his days contemplating the Green-Complexioned Adho-Mukhi, praying to her; twisting his body into odd positions, various geometric shapes, kandasana, the pose of the bulbous root, yogadandasana, the yogi's staff pose, strengthening his tendons, arteries, bones and internal organs. He practiced pious readings, taking meticulous care over the rules of syntax. He thrived on discomfort, inching his way closer to liberation through physical travail. By no means would he lean against a door-frame; never would he sit or sleep on a cushioned surface, preferring instead a bare, moss-free rock, an uneven bit of ground, a bed of granite, a pillow of thorns. And his austerities he performed as if they were sport, spending days on end standing on one leg with his eyes rolled back in his head, two days out of every week and a month out of every year fasting.

"I am like a piece of gold being purified by fire," he would tell himself with a certain degree of pride, considering his career to be that of a hero, a spiritual champion.

6. In Verona, in the church of Sant'Anastasia, there is a fresco by Pisanello depicting St. George. It is high up and difficult to see, but looking closely one can make out the teeth, small and somewhat sharp. Very blond hair. Skin extremely pale and a refined chin. Once this saint was chopped into numerous pieces, but came back to life. The reason for this is that he ate almost exclusively cinnamon, and by doing so gained the protection of a number of powerful spirits. It was they who sewed his body back together with invisible thread.

7. For her armpits she used a formula made from earth of the isle of Samos, balsam of opoponax, and rose juice. She anointed her ears with a mixture of spikenard juice, mastic, cariofilo, and storax grease. Her face was anointed with fenugreek flour, tragacanth, and star earth.

8. Daniel de Luxe, after performing a horrible deed, buried the razor blade in his back yard. It grew into a tree. Every time a bird lands on it, it gets sliced in two.

WILD DUCKS

1. Everyone is either too young, or too old.

2. He cut pictures of naked women out of dirty magazines and pinned them on the wall, claiming that they were all Kuan Yin.
Was he right?

3. Turnips aren't grown for their beauty.

4. He lay there, his head in a puddle of lavender oil, some primitive wing that could not stop flapping.

TISSUES AND BANNERS

1. Her mother would have done better to have given birth to a bottle of poison, a bag of scorpions, a famine—but instead this widow of a keeper of circus animals gave the world Theodora. The less said the better about her childhood, her upbringing, which was like maggot-infested flesh. It is well-known, anyhow, that in the Hippodrome where her father had displayed his bears, she performed promiscuous mime acts, exciting the entire populace of the city, making them grunt like pigs and laugh like monkeys. They clapped their hands and dribbled their wine. Later, she took to prostitution on a grand scale, showing herself an expert in the trade, seeming to enjoy it more than her customers, who came from all walks of life to let themselves be perverted by this young lamia, that flower of depravity who fed on their souls, made them drunk with lust and glad that they could empty their purses at her naked feet which danced about, arching, toes wiggling.

After eating a host of men,—of smiths, burly masons,

bakers with flour under their nails, shipwrights, historians, vintners, smelters, strong-shanked laborers, retired soldiers, new recruits, bald gynecologists, drunk carpenters and mariners—she finally fell in with the emperor himself. That he fell in love with her is no wonder. Wraith and unclean spirit go together. He was fascinated by all things evil in this world and wanted nothing better than to align himself with the worst possible mate.

The world had never known such a cruel woman—a woman who did away with her only son after he came begging her for help and who indeed made all decisions based on political expediency, self-preservation, and her own need for pleasure, filling her dungeons with shivering landowners whom she deprived of their fortunes while filling her bed with pornographic youths dredged up from the filthiest hovels of the city.

2. When he took his marriage vows, the bride insisted that he wet his mouth with the blood of a freshly killed chicken. He did this and, in fact, remained a faithful husband.

3. There was a man who, after many years of practice, finally was able to liquefy marble with his bare hands.
A useless skill.

4. A very brave soldier cut off his own head and walked over ten miles to present it to his king.

CONSTANT PRINCIPLE

1. At night I thought of the people I had met and realized I had met no one.

2. One day, while wandering with his begging bowl through the village, cow-like, in search of food, Madhusudan was assaulted by the smell of cooking flounder.

"Oh nose," he murmured, "repress yourself, from that object!"

A fleshy but pretty-featured woman, the wife of the village doctor, came walking with swift and delicate steps from her door, carrying a great clay pot in her hands. Madhusudan followed her with his eyes as she made her way down the street and then, curious as to where she could be rushing with such a succulent dish, followed her with his own feet . . . to the hut of Vishvatma!

And as the ascetic passed by he could hear that man's soft, cooing voice praising the succulence of the fish, so perfectly cooked in the milk of coconut and seasoned with coriander.

"What a gross fellow," the ascetic said to himself. "First he lays hands on a common harlot, and now he spends his forenoon meditating on the flavor of a fish!"

Madhusudan considered that his friend had indeed fallen from the path. But observing the sins of others is often as fascinating as dwelling on one's own virtues. And, for one reason or another, the ascetic daily found himself passing by the other's dwelling. At one time he saw Vishvatma fanning himself with the feather of a peacock, at another massaging his feet and rubbing them with palm-oil. What self-indulgence!

But as disgusting as this was to Madhusudan, it was nothing in comparison to the fame which he saw Vishvatma gradually acquiring; for the latter was becoming a magnet to disciples. They, young and old alike, crowded around their moon-faced and thick-lashed guru, laughing and joking, fruits and flowers piled high on each side and the air seasoned with incense.

"Vishvatma is a very holy man," he one day overheard a woman say to her neighbor.

"Yes," the other replied in solemn, respectful tones, "he is the most holy man in the district. What good fortune to have him near us!"

3. And so the women spent their days in the hall of the prison weaving the web, with nothing to support their constitutions but the merest crusts of bread. But then, at night, when they were forced back into their dark cell, other women arrived who, under instruction from the king, unraveled the work the princess and her handmaid

had done during the day, so that no progress was made.

"It seems that this web in no way nears completion though each day we work on it for a great many hours," Roma said one night to her mistress.

"Yes," Aemilia replied, "it deeply aggravates me, for I have been without the *hominem sine consortio* for many months and am thereby, as you can see, forced to *exercere manus meæ* in order to *satis eros* which *uritur in calidis* me from hour to hour. I only wish that by rubbing my belly in the same manner I could do away with hunger as well."

Now, while the princess was philosophizing over her own belly, the belly of Roma was growing larger with each day that passed; and then one morning, very early, she went into labor and was shortly thereafter delivered of two twin boys, the children of the phantom, extremely handsome and of a size somewhat more than that of ordinary babies.

Faustulus, who had been monitoring the young women closely, straightaway apprised the king of the situation.

"Destroy the children of this woman," Tarchetius commanded, "for I feel quite certain that, if they were to live, they would one day threaten my sovereignty."

The attendant then went to the prison, with every intention of carrying out the king's orders, though he inwardly lamented at having to perform such an immoral chore.

"I have been instructed to take the babies to a very respectable wet nurse," he told Roma. "You need have no fear for their safety, for the good woman is as strong as a chestnut tree, and carries in her healthy bosom as much milk as a well-grazed cow."

The young woman, with a mother's instinct, instantly suspected some sort of foul play, and prostrating herself before Faustulus said, "Dear sir, I feel quite confident that the king in no way wants these two boys of mine to live, for otherwise he would not have kept me imprisoned here for the past nine months. Undoubtedly their divine origin greatly frightens him. Yet, though you are the chief attendant of the king, would you for that reason not only sin against mankind (for what could be more brutal than infanticide), but also the very gods, whose instrument it surely was that impregnated me. Now I beg of you," she continued, *revelationem papillas*, which were *sicut nix* and very perfectly formed, "that you will refrain from this wicked deed and thereby secure yourself, not only the good will of the gods, but also my everlasting affection." With which words she began to *at illi amatorie*, touching with fingers lithe as a coil of snakes and pouting with lips red as crushed pomegranates, hoping in that way to advance her petition.

The Princess Aemilia, seeing this scene enacted before her, joined in the supplication without an instant's hesitation. Dexterously she disrobed and, with genuine avidity, added the offer of her own more experienced services to those of her handmaid, should Faustulus refrain from harming the children.

The attendant, being not different from all other men, was found to be a reasonable listener when confronted by such convincing arguments and very soon assured the ladies that he would in no way harm the children should they, the two women, agree to certain proposals of his, which he then laid forth in a spirited manner, informing them at the same time that if ever there were a conjuror able to fill two temples with a single idol, it was himself, a fact which they should not ignore in their deliberations. This idol of his, now *durabilis* as any bronze or marble, and raised to a position where it could be easily worshipped, *excelsum excitata mulieres conveniunt*. He then, after requesting them to *situm corporum* in attitudes of due reverence, proceeded to show Aemilia and Roma that it was not the gods alone who could fling hot bolts of thunder and smash through Olympus, but that certain mortal men were also able to work divinely heroic deeds, boost women atop the heavenly pinnacle and make them *attulit in gemitu*. Indeed, it must be said that all three together experienced the most delicious pleasures that humans could, Faustulus relishing with dynamic lips and tongue the *dulces ambrosiae mulierum*, while they in turn were well pleased to enjoy the succulent offerings of his overflowing horn-of-plenty.

Having tasted the bounty of such fertile gardens, and eager to reap many more harvests in the future, Faustulus then took the children away, but instead of dispatching them laid the young beings on the bank of the river Tiber, in an area frequented by many washerwomen, where he believed they would be discovered in no short time and most certainly be provided for. Things turned out differently, however, as it was not a washerwoman that came upon the babies, but a she-wolf, who took them up in her jaws, carried them to her den and gave them suck. A woodpecker also brought morsels of food, berries and crumbs of bread snatched from the nearby town, and put them into their mouths, so that the little boys in no way lacked nutrition. Then one day a cowherd caught sight of the children and witnessed the manner in which they were being cared for by the she-wolf and the woodpecker. After recovering from his astonishment, he approached the she-wolf's den, took the children in his arms and brought them to his own home. And so they were saved, and when they were grown men, they set upon King Tarchetius and overcame him.

4. Vishvatma would spend his mornings in the temple of the deity, gazing at her in rapture. In the afternoon he would receive the ever-increasing disciples who, because of him, brought numerous offerings to the Green-Complexioned Adho-Mukhi—great ripe and fragrant mangoes, desserts made from honey and rice, shakarpara and red bean pudding. Affluent merchants gave melon seeds swimming in syrup, wealthy donor-ladies gave sweetened cream of buffalo milk seasoned with cardamom powder—and of course much of this found its way into Vishvatma's hut, where it was distributed amongst those present.

"Everyone gives sweets," he would say. "Do they know how partial I am to sweets?"

And he would proceed to sink his teeth into a piece of fried and sugared cheese, flavored with rose oil, while a mellow-voiced youth sang a devotional song to the sound of an expert musician playing the sitar.

These sights made Madhusudan all the more adamant for his own practice, and his asceticism reached fever pitch. Day by day he grew more lean and fierce-looking. His hair was a nest of mats that writhed like snakes every time he turned his head. His finger and toe nails were perilously long, curling like shavings of wood. He never took ablutions, and by no means would he rub his body with scented powder or do anything whatsoever to pamper it. Instead he spent his time practicing penance in the cremation grounds, braving the smell of burning flesh, roasting himself in the blazing heat of the summer sun.

5. Madhusudan sat somewhat ostentatiously in the midst of a clearing adjacent to the temple, his body twisted in the dwi pada sirsasana, with feet interlocked behind head and palms of hands pressed together at the chest. Hearing a sound, he opened his eyes and looked up, aroused himself from his contemplation. A column of elephants was making its way along the road, toward the temple, the elongated upper lips of the animals marvelous, their tusks of ivory pretty, their bodies richly caparisoned, backs saddled with howdahs. To each side of them strode attendants, and behind a number of palanquins were carried by strong-shouldered men.

It was obviously the train of some royal personage. Madhusudan, upon seeing this sight, let his face become all the more grave, his posture all the more perfect. A number of people from the party seemed to be taking notice of him. He heard their voices and saw their gazes fixed in his direction. An attendant broke away from the train and sprinted forward.

"Ah, finally," the ascetic said to himself. "Vishvatma might have merchants, but the royalty comes to me."

"Excuse me," said the attendant, approaching, "but could you direct me to the residence of the renowned and blessed Vishvatma? My master, King T——, sorely wants to meet that great yogi!"

With an outstretched and quivering finger Madhusudan pointed the way to the other's hut . . . followed with his eyes the noble walk of those slow-moving creatures . . . then with his mind envisioned the king bowing humbly at the feet of plump Vishvatma, those feet that had transported that woman, that heavily-perfumed prostitute . . .

The ascetic's concentration was broken; his mind confused. He rose to his feet.

"Well," he murmured, as he walked away, his head hanging low, "Vishvatma might be gaining worldly fame—but that has nothing to do with spiritual accomplishment. If these people only knew . . ."

HOLDING UP THE SKY

1. Arnaldus de Villa Nova, the first man to distil pure alcohol, together with Jaime de Toledo would go about inviting young and healthy men to their studios and killing them. This they only did in the months of April and May. They drained the blood from their victims and, mixing it with fruit juices and extracts of certain flowers, made a distillation. With this substance, they were able to revive the dead, but only for about twenty minutes.

2. Erotic places:
    Ears.
    Throat.
    Armpits.
    Lips.
    Thighs.
    Stomach.
    Breasts.
    Elbows.

3. He who had dedicated his life to the pursuit of contemplative ideals and extreme practices of self-denial, threw himself down before the Green-Complexioned Adho-Mukhi, pushed his face against the floor; and she looked on, frozen, without the least show of life or emotion. That evening he recited her mantra ten thousand times, trying to hide with his prayers the persistent image—of that loose woman being carried through the water, mounted on Vishvatma's back. His indignation would not leave him. In his mind that moon-faced fellow was, by his very presence, soiling the temple of the deity. He, Madhusudan, was sanitary. And was it not his duty to see that the temple was clean and that the Green-Complexioned Adho-Mukhi was only worshipped by the righteous?

The next day, before the sun had yet risen, he rose from his hard resting place and stalked, evenly and with due caution, toward the temple which rose up like a great black mound, the numerous carvings which decorated its exterior barely discernible, like so many ghosts. On his way, he caught site of Vishvatma, who was just making his way from the stepwell, where he had been performing his morning ablutions. Madhusudan could hear him singing softly to himself, in a voice childishly sweet, though to the ascetic more obnoxious than the buzz of any mosquito. He saw Vishvatma make his way to the temple, up its steps and through its door. A shiver coursed through the ascetic's spine, a feeling filled his head, a strong feeling of belligerence, extreme aversion, aroused by the nearness of that plump fellow who was praised by all, who had people from the highest grades of life humble themselves at his feet even though his hands were contaminated. And those hands were now going to make offering to the deity, to the deity that Madhusudan worshipped, the Green-Complexioned Adho-Mukhi whose image he must indeed protect.

The ascetic felt flames rise to his cheeks and a red haze clouded his sight. Not a few steps distant was the hut of a thatch cutter, and from his doorpost hung the machete of his trade. Madhusudan picked up the tool and made his way toward the temple, slowly mounted the steps, his thoughts uncontrolled, a mixture of violent conceptions and sordid images. With wild, vengeful eyes he looked through the door. Inside he saw Vishvatma, sitting innocently on the floor, his broad mouth cloven into a smile. There before the man was her, the Green-Complexioned Adho-Mukhi, that genetrix and destroyer of all things, now not merely a statue of carved wood, but fully animate, dancing, her anklets tinkling, her feet, body, both moving rhythmically in a pattern of steps, with slight leaps, skips; hands, hastas, now picking ketaki flowers, now strewing the air with the smell of sandal-wood, casting shadows of severe sunlight and rays of darkness, each of her steps scattering ever-effulgent stars, luminaries, into the indefinitely great three-dimensional expanse, her arms embracing time and space, lips saying secret mystical things.

The tool, the weapon, fell from Madhusudan's hand. He felt his skin grow cold and become textured with goose bumps. A peacock cried in the near distance; and the ascetic heard sounds of astonishment and praise flow from his own mouth as he burst through the opening; and the Green-Complexioned Adho-Mukhi became stationary—was once again unmoving wood.

Madhusudan collapsed at Vishvatma's feet, anointed them with his tears.

"Madhusudan!" Vishvatma exclaimed with some surprise.

"Vishvatma, it is truly you who are the holy man and I the rodent. The Green-Complexioned Adho-Mukhi knows you. She dances for you." And the tears ran down his hollow cheeks. "Yet I can't understand it. I, so very appropriate in my every action. You, living in a heap of mighty lapses."

"Well, I do enjoy my sweets."

"But you . . . who touched . . . facilitated a harlot!"

Vishvatma looked at the ascetic somewhat gravely.

"It is true Madhusudan that long ago I took a woman upon my back—a woman who needed help. But soon after I took her up, I set her down, I placed her on the other side of the road. The reality is that I viewed her as nothing more than a sack of flesh and bones. But you, what did you view her as? For, all these years later, you still carry her with you wherever you go. And thus your soul is restless, like a palm tree swept by a gust of the wind. Attachment really is the murderer of friendship."

4. He was an effeminate fellow, catamite by trade—a young man who spent his days lurking about the Hippodrome, his nights submerged in peals of laughter, completely wet with wine.

When he danced, he was neither serious nor decorous, anything but, grinning as he displayed his deft footwork, while the harp and flute went at high speed, his hips swinging this way and that, in tabulated confusion, like some hallucinating goat bounding through a labyrinth. And then, after tipping a half-jar of wine down his throat, he would take up the cymbals, frolic around the room. He was indeed an expert at the geranos, and old lechers would stick to him in abundance, so that he was always able to stick his bread in honey.

RED DALMATICS

1. Meeting beings wandering the desolate earth, hungry and alone, he offered them liquid from the palms of his hands, but they gnawed the flesh from his fingers, with puckered lips sucked the marrow from his bones.

2. Marino D'Acquaviva, Duke of Olona, finished his meal of fennel soup, tongue savory and cutlets of wild boar, drained his glass of vino de Marcha, and rose from the table.

"Lazzaro," he said to a servant who stood waiting by the door, "I will study tonight; see that a fire is lighted in the library."

"My lord," the man replied with a bow, "in anticipation of the event, I have already done so."

D'Acquaviva climbed the stairs to that chamber, two walls of which were covered with volumes, hundreds of them, as well as numerous rare manuscripts unbound. A third wall, in which sat the great fireplace, was frescoed almost entirely black and dark blue, with a moon rising over a strange and haunted landscape. The fourth side of the room was lined with windows, which looked out onto the piazza below, where a group of youths stood in conversation, muffling their laughter as best they could. The duke locked the door of the room, closed the shutters of the windows, all but one, and took down a notebook from his shelves. He then set a chair near the fireplace, and sat down.

"Lazzaro has not made this fire quite what it should be," he murmured to himself. He removed the grate and tossed on a number of logs, which shortly began to crackle and burst into flame.

With a grotesque smile he now opened a notebook, which was bound in stiff, white pig's skin, well-oiled and smooth to the touch. Within were the recipes, those of Abu Musa Djaber ibn Hayan El Azder El Kufi, which he had had translated—broken into bits and had translated by numerous scholars, each of which was entrusted with but a portion, so none but he ever saw the whole. Those pages contained much secret knowledge:

Item. To make a commotion at your pleasure.
Item. To make a flood in a dry ground.
Item. To cause war amongst fishes, fouls, and such like.
Item. To make a man think he is in a place where he is not.
Item. To cause thunder and lightning.
Item. To fly your spirit from its frame.

It was to this last he turned, as he had on many nights during those past months, his eyes glittering as he read once more over that most special business, that made it so he might sneak without weight and be without body.

He read: "Hermes said of thimiamate, of the Moon is cinnamon, lignum aloes, mastic, crocus, costus, maces, and myrtle. We put this that each planet has a part in it." And then taking from his breast a sachet of those herbs, he tossed a pinch upon the flames, which instantly began to smoke, with an ominous rosy color, and the room was filled with a most foreign perfume.

He read: "With due knowledge of this power, region, without form or taste, you wilt do thus . . ." And then the formula, the meditation. At the base of the spine he began, to prod, enchant, and then work his consciousness upward, through the stomach, then heart, throat, the zones of thought and vision; and white-hot his spirit burst from its cage and flew through the crown of his head. Below he saw that body, elegantly attired, with a pale and noble face—that form now left without ideas, feelings or wishes, before the blazing, smoke-spitting fire. But there was the bond that he might return again, and he now had the freedom for the night to go where he pleased, unencumbered by a physical frame.

Out the window he blew, lighter than wind, as supple as the very air. There was the February night, black, cold and clear, and he could hear them, those youths of the piazza, and he did spy on their talk, which was lies of love conquests and other such things.

"Mere ants that crawl this earth," his thoughts went,

slipping through the sky like some vapor.

He sped upward, over the church, that building he had spent much money to see adorned with marble statues and colorful frescoes—for he was lord of the town, and would have it so. He was lord of the sleepy dark town below him, which had become a nest where he could breed his magic in peace and cultivate those arcane arts which let him now slip through the bedrooms of the village maidens, him as incubus, a brilliant ephemera of filth that left behind slithering trails of Paphian nightmares. That spirit hissed through the trees, through the surrounding forest, and he did secretly watch, perlustrate, hear and laugh with noiseless ferocity at his own power, and the weakness of the tenants around him.

There was a country girl, not yet of her sixteenth year. She was the daughter of a pollaiolo, a dealer in chickens and eggs, and to her he went, watched as she undressed her extremely pale and not altogether rude body. He prodded her mouth with his airy tongue, a muscle of evil thought, and did press upon those sharp little teeth and subsequently explore the nether regions of her virgin frame, enjoying the blush that came to her and the slight whine that escaped her lips.

He would have never found such pleasure by simply dirtying her with the meat of his physical body.

Then it was into the yard to frighten the dog and make him howl; through the chicken coops to harass the birds, make them cackle, beat their wings and spring from their roosts, agitate them so that they would not lay eggs for weeks to come. And across to the hamlet of a widow he now flew, to fill her sleeping time with nightmares, and the soft caress of fear as he snuggled against her full naked form.

And so the hours passed, with dishonorable investigations, and pride in his uncanny skill, until he knew it to be time to return from that sport, to re-inhabit his own noble body which undoubtedly sat before a fire now grown cold. Up and over he went, and danced across the sharp tops of pines and neared the nucleus of Olona, which was, though, strangely aglow for that time of night.

"What is this?" he soundlessly murmured, and jetted with all the more speed toward the town.

In the piazza there were many people gathered. Men, short of breath, ran from the fountain to his, the Duke of Olona's, palazzo—the top story of which was alive with orange flames.

"It is the library," one man said. "The library has been set ablaze!"

"My manuscripts!" was the first idea that came to that spirit of Marino D'Acquaviva.

Waves of heat swept over the piazza and there were echoes of crackling, crashing timber.

"The poor Duke," Lazzaro cried as he ran frantically from the door, sparks dazzling behind him. "We cannot save the sleeping Duke!"

That spirit was then struck, by the words, the realization—for more than just the manuscripts were burning—his very body was engulfed in tongues of fire. And outside, watching, were the ideas, the feelings, the fear, to drift upon the wind, voiceless and incorporeal.

BEWILDERMENT

1. "Where?" Professor Gordon demanded. "Where is it?"

"This way," the boy replied once again. "This way, sir."

"No. No more 'this way, this way.' Where is it? Where–Is–It?"

"Devi this way, sir." The boy smiled. "Right this way."

It seemed obvious to Professor Gordon that he was getting nowhere. For hours he had wandered around the acid boglands which existed near the small Indian town of Bharatpur, his guide a young local who spoke but a few words of English. At first, when the youngster had indicated that he knew the location of the Devi, Professor Gordon had been overjoyed. He followed him along the built-up trails that led through the high grass. Once a python was pointed out with vehemence, but this, a mere reptile, was not what he had come for. The hours dragged on, he grew tired and angry, and still the boy shouted, "This way, this way!" It was obnoxious.

"Enough!" Professor Gordon cried, flinging a few rupees at his guide. "I am going back. You are no good. You are a bad guide. Bad guide!"

He knew it made little difference, as far as the other's comprehension went, how adamantly he uttered his words. The boy simply smiled, picked up the notes, and continued saying, "This way, this way," as he watched the middle-aged American disappear around a bend in the trail.

Was it an objective unattainable after all; just another fairy tale? He did not know. The environment was certainly plausible for the pitcher plant, and if there were seventy-three known species, why should not he root out a seventy-fourth? After all, the *Brocchinia reducta* had just been discovered a short while before, as well as Cantley's red. Gordon was certainly a better scholar than Cantley. Any reader of his *Cytotaxonomic Study of Sarraceniaceae of the Upper Americas* knew that much.

Trails criss-crossed each other all through the high swamp grass. There were no definite landmarks to get his bearings by, the terrain an even, unmodified morass. Off in the distance, a group of tribals gathered bundles of the tall grass, which they would later use for the construction of huts. The group was made up mostly of young women, who all waved to Professor Gordon as he passed. From where he stood, they looked somewhat attractive; their pendulous petals and buxom bracts; and he let out a sigh as he left them in his wake. It was not that they were more enticing than the sweet trumpet or black-eyed sundew, but there was something appealing about their native simplicity. It was a shame that he did not know their tongue, and was thus prevented from asking a few explicit questions pertaining to his quest.

His body exuded an uncomfortable degree of perspiration. The humidity, the thick air, did not make for a pleasant stroll. An occasional cloud of gnats blocked his path, and bit as he made his way through their midst. As he walked, he undid the water bottle from his pouch. Lifting it high, he let a jet stream into his open, upturned mouth. Unfortunately, while concentrating on the refreshment, he was distracted from the path before him. His foot landed in a pothole. He tripped and tumbled forward. When he sat up, a bruise blemished his forehead, secreting a few drops of blood. His glasses lay before him, one lens smashed, an arm broken off, beyond immediate repair. In a spasm of childish rage he flung them from him, and then clawed about, half blind, on the lonely dirt trail.

Before the occurrence, when his sight was unhampered, he had been still uncertain as to the most expedient path back to the main road. Now, vision blurred, head throbbing from the fall, he could not have pointed out so much as the correct direction, let alone the exact route.

"It doesn't matter about the glasses," he told himself in an aggravated voice. "I have a spare pair in my luggage at the guest house. Finding my way back is the obvious priority."

Doggedly he moved along the paths between the high grass, choosing by guesswork when a fork opened up before him. He was miserable and feeling the first twinges of desperation. A thin drizzle began to seep from the sky.

How he then longed to see a flock of those local maidens; to be taken back to some simple hut and fed a hot broth, or a cup of sweet tea. But the country around him seemed abandoned, the stillness only broken by the cry of a far-off bird, the splash of a frog entering the water; the backdrop a continuous pulsating of insect life.

Off in the distance he descried a canopy of apparent verdure. The drizzle thickened, and the liquid began to course down his face and saturate his clothes.

"At least those trees should offer me some shelter," he mumbled to himself, and jogged along the path that, to him, seemed the most direct, slipping in the rapidly forming mud as he went.

When he finally neared his destination, he was short of breath. His legs were splattered with mud, and his clothes clung to his awkward body. The thin hair of his head streaked down upon his face like limp weeds.

He hurried toward the inflorescent mantle of growth, relieved to see shelter so near, blurred as it might be. The leaves, yellowish-green, looking as great blades might, would offer the ideal shelter, and permit him some much-needed rest until the rain subsided.

He clung to the coarse trunk, pushing the hair back from his forehead and wiping extraneous liquid from his eyes and face.

"Maybe this tree does not offer quite adequate shelter, after all," he said, noting that his right foot rested in a fair-sized puddle.

The quaint hood, with its bright yellow tusks, hovered above his leg. There was the lip-like edge, the morbid and puckered peristome surrounding the fluid deposit. Attempting to remove his limb, he realized that it was held fast by the plant's gluey mucilage. The situation was palpable.

"Well," he said, smiling grimly as he noted the acute pain caused by the digestive enzymes and bristling trichomes, "Cantley might have his red, but I apparently have the *Gordonthes amputatio*. Or it has me."

2. Abstract as a nodding head.

Red as an old thumb stuck in a hole.

Pretentious as a clean-shaven poet some narrow bastard in new clothes with money to spare.

Dynamite is as soft as a lamb.

Loneliness is round.

3. Emperor Ming of Wei was involved in many wars and probably was fond of violence. One thing he was certainly not fond of was music. The sound of the moon guitar would anger him. He would become furious when he heard the ceremonial flute mount the scale of the phoenix. Instead he liked the sound of shrieks, and the sound of pounding. He had the wives of thousands of his citizens confiscated and, with a smile on his face, listened to their wailing. He set up building projects all around his palace and would listen happily to the sound of the mallets as they hammered away day and night.

4. The pear tree in the backyard was blossoming and it was a beautiful spring day, with the sky almost cloudless, and the surrounding high desert country peaceful and tainted green. The goat chewed at the new grass as the two men stood near, talking.

"Yes, he is a nice animal," said Dagoberto, his eyes shining from his tough, wrinkled face. "Fat around the ribs."

"You think it will be much trouble?" Peter asked deferentially.

"No, not for me. You are not used to it, but for me it's alright."

Peter nodded his head. He knew that the old man had done many such things in his time, and to him it was more or less routine. That was why he had asked him over, to find out what it was all about. From someone who knew.

Ada, Peter's wife, looked out from the window. It made her queasy to see them standing there talking, as the goat calmly grazed. If she had known his intentions, she would not have let Peter buy it.

Reading, her eyes took in the words, but her mind did not register them. She still heard the voices; Dagoberto's rough, accented; and Peter's, always interspersed with a nervous little laugh. She wondered if he even remembered all the times she had taken leftovers and bits of old bread and vegetables out to the goat, and how she always smiled and laughed at its big, round eyes.

There was the bleating—strange how sedate, considering that the old man's hands must be gripping—and

131

Peter holding it down. The task would be done very quickly, the knife entering, slashing the lovely throat, and the very warm blood, still living—it floods and saturates the ground. Like a puddle of syrup. And Peter still laughing nervously. Dagoberto still calm. The eyes, big and round, still open.

She slammed the book shut and threw it aside. Was that the goat crying? It was hard to tell. Being actually distraught, she was unsure of her senses. She ran to the window.

Peter had his arms stretched up to the pear tree; Dagoberto was crouched on the ground. He held a rag in one hand and was working at something in the other. Peter stepped back. The goat hung from the tree. A rich fluid ran from it, with emission, the turgescence, and the twitching.

The white blossoms were red, and later Dagoberto would return to supervise the butchering of the animal, in return for a few choice cuts, as well as the kidneys, heart, tongue, brains and sweetbreads.

5. The odor emanating from the kitchen genuinely disgusted Ada.

Peter had diced a number of onions and sautéed them in the bottom of a large pot, adding chunks of the cut-up goat, which were a dark, brownish red, and heavily marbled with fat. He braised them and then added two cans of whole, peeled tomatoes, fresh celery, carrots and green chiles, and, later, frozen corn. He let it cook for almost two hours, on a high heat, occasionally adding spices, and water, to keep it from burning.

Ada opened all the windows in the house, and sat near one, looking out at the overlying hills and the blue, clean sky beyond. She watched as her husband went from his desk to the kitchen, where he stirred and tasted, and then back to the desk, to resume his work.

Later, when the table was set, she sat in bleak expectation, a sympathetic smile plastered on her face. She could hear Peter in the kitchen, as he clattered around and whistled.

"Carne de chivo!" he said, setting a steaming bowl in front of Ada, and another at his place.

She claimed that it looked wonderful. She lifted a spoonful of the broth to her lips, blew on it, and tasted. He asked if it was good and she said it was, though she did not think so.

Peter took in several spoonfuls of broth and vegetables, and then began to pick out chunks of meat with his fingers, gnawing at them and sucking on the bones. It was obvious that he thoroughly relished it, which seemed utterly obscene to Ada, who found the dish to be the most nauseating she had ever tried.

Peter's lips were greasy. He said she should eat some of the meat.

She fished out a small piece with her spoon, put her lips around it, and then set it between her teeth. The flesh resisted such delicate advances. She tore a few fibers off and chewed them obediently. Peter had already finished his bowl; a small pile of bones and gristle sat on the napkin at his place; he returned to the kitchen for seconds. She quickly got up from her seat and chucked the contents of her bowl out the open window, then grabbed a few of the bones from Peter's place and put them near hers.

"More?" he asked when he returned.

"No, thank you. It was very good."

After the meal, she watched as her husband ran his tongue over his gums, and between his teeth, dislodging strands of the goat.

SACRED CONTOURS

1. There was once a king who gave the poor power over the rich. But this was in a different world.

2. It is best not to call a thief a thief.

3. There is a certain village where, instead of beds, people sleep on tortoises.

4. I stood at the edge of the clearing. I wanted to smoke a cigarette, but did not dare. It was dark and I was wearing a dark blue suit and did not want to be seen, could not be seen.
After I had stood there for about an hour they started coming, at first just two or three, but soon there were a good forty, maybe fifty of them. Some carried flashlights and then others lit torches so the whole clearing was filled with light.
Everyone was wearing a mask. Some looked like grotesque birds with long square beaks, others pigs or

insect-like entities with fangs, carrying rattles and tiny little drums that they tapped on with their index fingers.

I stepped further back. I could not be seen. Not that I was frightened—you do not get frightened at things like that and I had almost known what to expect anyhow.

They started singing and, one by one, were grabbed up by a short man with a beard and put in a pot. He drank them and then fell back exhausted. His body was the color of a rainbow.

5. Peas and beans were beginning to climb the string trellis set up along the fence, and lettuce grew in front of these, some light green and very succulent of appearance, another variety with bronzy, red leaves, forming a row of lovely rosettes. The tomato plants they had bought from a nursery in town and planted in the sunniest spot out back, in wire cages. They were doing very well, and already had blossoms, and very small green tomatoes. Ada worked around them with a trowel, occasionally looking over at Peter, who was busy near the pear tree, where he had planted a fairly large patch of orach. She had told him that it was too shady there to plant anything, but he had just shrugged his shoulders and proceeded to turn the earth. Now the plants, each set about fourteen inches apart, were already about a foot tall. The leaves were a vivid maroon color, which Ada should have found beautiful, but did not.

"It is just like him," she told herself, "to plant something that I have never even heard of, and have no interest in, instead of something nice, like spinach or broccoli. And there, of all places."

"Nice tomato plants," were the hoarse words that made her look up.

Dagoberto stood leaning over the fence, a hand-rolled cigarette burning between his thick fingers and his face shaded by an old cowboy hat. Even his smile, to Ada, expressed something aside from good will. When they had first met him she thought he was charming, picturesque. Now she felt an aversion to him. She remembered him carrying away the kidneys, heart, tongue, brains and sweetbreads wrapped up in an old newspaper,—and she remembered what had spilled.

"Already getting some green ones," he continued.

"Yes, it won't be long before they are ripe."

Later, sitting in the bedroom and reading a book, she tried hard not to hear the sound of their voices, as they drank cans of beer in the yard.

6. The freezer was full of the meat. Peter seemed to subsist on it. Ada got out of eating the substance by claiming that it did not agree with her digestion. She burned incense, foot after foot, in an attempt to cover an odor which was ominous to her. Reminding her of what was worst in man. Or even schoolboys, who find pleasure in the torture of insects and lower animals.

The orach was the only vegetable Peter touched in the garden. He made salads of it, dressing it with soy sauce, garlic, olive oil and vinegar; and later, when the plants were about two feet tall, he boiled the dark maroon leaves and ate them with just salt, pepper and apple cider vinegar. The skull still hung from a branch of the pear tree; now partly covered by foliage, it was true—but it was there, it could be seen—even in the dark, a stroke of white.

He growled and smiled, eyes twinkling slits.

7. That summer Ada spent a good deal of time wandering in the low hills around where they lived. Peter did not work well when she was around. He would drift from room to room in the adobe house, in a gloomy stupor, his face looking sharp and unpleasant. At other times he was frankly a nuisance—giving unwanted caresses in the morning, and early afternoon hours.

And summer thrust itself into autumn.

She walked along the ridge that rose up behind their house. To the north she could see the higher mountains, the summit covered with aspens which were already starting to turn slightly golden; and to the south, the hills dropped away into canyons and arroyos; and further off there were mesas, in the high desert.

As she walked she scanned the ground for arrowheads and thought about how nice it would be to be up in that higher altitude, wandering in the shade of those big trees. She turned and looked down into the valley below. A thick vein of green ran through there; the stream, which wound by their house, grown thickly with cottonwood trees and Russian olives. She could see the house itself, looking very small, the yard dotted with the lime green of the garden, the pear tree, and that dark red streak. She imagined him inside, at his desk, presumably hard at work.

She walked down the other side of the ridge, past piñon trees, yucca and stands of cholla cactus; down into the ravine which was based with pink rock and sand. She usually simply went up the other side of the ravine, but this time she moved along it, letting it guide her course. A gun shot echoed out of the hills. She continued, making her way through the dry gulch.

Ada came around a bend and sat down on a rock in a small patch of shade. She opened her water bottle, lifting it to her dry lips. The voices were there, though she could not make out what they said. She noticed, over by a piñon tree on an opposite hill, the two men.

She knew right away that one of them was Dagoberto, but it was not until a few moments later that she recognized the other as Peter. It was obvious that they did not see her, and she watched as they dealt with the dead jackrabbit. Peter held it by the hind legs while Dagoberto cut at the fur at the joint, and pulled the skin away from the legs, turning it inside out like a glove. He then severed the head and threw it aside with the skin, and proceeded to gut it, removing the entrails and casting them aside, except one handful, possibly the heart and liver, which he tucked away in a handkerchief.

She remained very still, the water bottle tightly gripped in both hands. Dagoberto held the dead animal by the forepaws, and the two men disappeared, walking down toward the valley. She could hear the sound of their voices and low laughs, and did not move until the ravens came and pecked at the remains, and the buzzards circled overhead.

8. Staircases, catacombs, pits, endless falls, luxurious screams.

9. The man across from her had sallow cheeks, and deep-set eyes, and was not in the least bit silent about eating his supper. He slurped up the vegetable, the maroon juice tainting his mouth, and chewed, almost ravenously, at the bones of goat.
She fell asleep in a chair, with a book in her hand.
Wounds, superficial, were inflicted with forks, scissors, thorny branches, etc. That they continued to laugh was, of course, no surprise to her. Fastening the eyelids with the eyelashes—and the hide, which was rough, even with its soft hair.
She got up and went to the bedroom. He was not there, though the bed was in disorder and his clothes littered the floor. There were sounds from the yard, and she saw, when she went to the window, that the moon was brilliant.
In the orach, beneath the pear tree, which was like an outstretched hand, he clawed—naked, quadrupedal, and half obscured by the dark red leaves.

GIGGLING FLUTES

1. She cried out like a peacock and then pecked away at his lips like a sparrow.

2. He saw her. She was intelligent, healthy. He visited with her in red. Listened with the ears of a connoisseur. A few disconnected phrases climbed off his tongue.

3. Looking at the ground, he saw scattered, fallen leaves.

4. In his youth the bait had tasted sweet, candy-coated gore, and lines read in raw innocence—seeds than blew in from some unknown region, some planet, coldly grim and lifeless. He had taken in such tales, as they were, interweeded with adventure, jauntily expressing the fears that make men reluctant to step outside when day falls dark and prompts them to keep secure behind bolted doors; safety only corporeal, so false. Those Gothic novellas and other, Romantic narratives of restless, hyperbolic spirits had been his nursing breast.

Andy went without to trek the fields or drop a line for fish in a stagnant pool.

Omit not your studies pleasurable for the easy apex of mundane, circumferent sky.

And so the youth, with glittering, gem-like eyes, burrowed into the public house of books, emerging as the sun shed its last drops of blood on the western sky, frail back bent with bursting sack. In a room decorated with a sole reproduction (torn-out cardboard cover) by Dürer, a knight making his way through a heart-shivering, beast-seething landscape.

He entered inferior worlds where some impaler strummed upon his beef-red nerves.

The dog barked outside his window.

Blacker than veins of subterranean coal the back of a big beetle looking for a place to cling to. Trembling claw imitated, in mirror uneven and dexterous in its deception.

In between lettering he read, in between reading he lettered (pages appearing as if dirtied by muddy sparrows' feet). He grew without human contact; grew psychically, through the disturbing splashes, which stung worse than proboscis of bee. The moon dribbled its melancholy light through the window sashes and drowned him in its waxy bath. A shadow moved past the back door.

He crept through his portal, glad to avoid the radiance of sun. He went through the gridded, pitch-stroked streets. His true hair turned the shade of iron. His lips became pinched and chin corrugated, a few stray globs of flesh protruding from it. Venturing without, for revictualization, he disguised himself in a wig and paint, in no way wanting to see his countenance inscribed on the eyeballs of others. Home again. Worship in solitude. A recitation of iron bells.

Outside, clouds swam like jellyfish through the starless sky. The dog trotted off, panting, tongue lolling, and Andy followed at its side. Through the sleeping streets they walked, to the city's edge and then through the whispering glades beyond.

"Where to?" Andy asked. But the dog simply moved on, without reply, its paws patting softly on the ground.

Soon they reached a range of rusted fencing and proceeded along its edge, apparently in search of an opening. The shadows were thick on the other side and the country invisible. Andy pressed his fingers against his own fleshless ribs and felt a pulsating heart. One eye white, the other blue, the canine looked up, its gums black, tinged with wounded red. The gate swung open with a sad creak.

And through, into the other side he went, to the place of his ugly dreams, his feet treading on, sending shudders through the web of tensely bleak fibers and bundles of fibers, summoning creatures unbound, maleficent combinations of deep-rooted, other-worldly alarms—things which are left unmentioned, and tortures which, destroying every hope, should not be whispered.

His screech escaped through a distended, peanut-shaped orifice.

WORN-OUT STRAW SANDALS

1. There was a temple, high in the mountains. When devotees went there, a mongoose would approach them and vomit pearls into their hands.

2. He poured whisky into the glass, lifted it to his lips, tipped it back and swallowed. Everyone was surprised when he fell down with a hole in his head.

3. Quiet things:
    A piece of driftwood.
    Worms.
    A flute with no holes.
    Boiled asparagus.
    The mouth on the back of a person's head.

4. There was a man who painted a very beautiful picture.
"That is awful," said his friend.

GENERATING WORLDS

1. Countess de Báthory exuded a sigh and lay back, letting the warmth of the rich liquid subdue the anxiety of her limbs. There was no question as to its superior quality. That of the peasants lacked the luster of this new stock, with its coral-like shading, when seen, a few beads at a time, trickling through the network of her fingers. Sitting in that dainty marble tub was like being immersed in a bath of liquefied jasper, or juice of ruby. How much better it was than that blackish goo, by-product of the masses! And there was always the question whether in truth those young hussies, brought up on their turnips and mutton fat, were the half of them virgins after all. How much better these twenty fresh dames, having never supped upon anything more base than a roasted sparrow, or a slightly over-developed lettuce leaf.

"Here is a heater," Dorotta said, making her way through the mammoth oaken door girt with studded brass bands. Smiling with the deference of the well-fed toady, she approached, a splashing pail dangling from the crook of her arm, her obscenely ugly form taking on the hue of moldy cheese by the flicker of the candelabra light.

"Is that the last of them?" the countess asked wearily.

"Yes, the Princess Gina, she did struggle so, m'Lady. You'd think the iron maiden was some kind of unheard of monstrosity by the way she protested."

"Well, the aristocracy, for all their breeding, are often rather naïve," the countess commented with a pout.

"A goblet?"

"Naturally. You know how I savor the bouquet."

Dorotta, having fetched a vessel of blue crystal from a nearby cabinet, ladled off a delicate portion from the bucket, offering it up to her mistress with all the grace at her command. Countess de Báthory let five of her languorous white tentacles enwrap the colorful cup and, with the quivering lips of a voluptuary, drained it posthaste, her eyes fluttering back in her head, as in marked ecstasy.

"How is it, m'Lady?"

"Oh . . . Gina!" the countess muttered, throwing her head back in a half-swoon.

"Yes, a sweet girl," chuckled Dorotta and began to slowly empty the pail around the alabaster form of her mistress.

"Save an itcze or two for the cellar," the countess commanded. She sunk herself down to her chin in the dimpling red bath. "And make sure you mince this one properly. I don't fancy having cumbersome pieces of evidence lying around. People always get worked up over little princesses."

Dorotta, having kept her office in the castle for a good number of years, knew the stamp of dismissal well. With a small amount of the liquid still oscillating in the bottom of the bucket, she made her departure, through the mammoth oaken door girt with studded brass bands, down the hall of imperious stone lit by torchlight, to the nether-winding stairway, which she descended, with the heavy steps of the cave dweller, as was her way. The chamber, set far below the level of the earth, was typical of morbid Hungarian tyrants: a rack, an array of metallic instruments of torture, one or two pots of boiling oil, a red-hot poker installed handily in the flames—the usual ensemble of macabre paraphernalia.

Having set down the bucket, she undid the buckles of the iron maiden, kicking aside the spout which emerged from its base. She pulled at the pressed and disenfranchised figure within, dislodging it from the points which had forced its soul's departure.

"The trouble m'Lady goes to . . . just to stave off a few wrinkles," Dorotta grumbled, flinging the stained petal of lily over one shoulder with an obvious measure of disdain.

She made her way toward higher ground, at first retracing her morbid steps, and then traversing other halls and ascending other steps, until her bulk appeared at the top of the southeastern parapet of the castle, like some fiend against the midnight sky.

"Let the wolves do the mincing," she hissed and

raised the limp figure on high, flinging it into the swallow of black space before her.

2. The crisp of morning. Ribbons of mist. Bundled in roughly-hewn sheep skin and garments of hemp, the group of illiterate peasants gathered around the drained and naked body, their faces arranged in wonder and grave compassion. How much like their own daughters she was, though her hands were without callus and limbs of a daintier build. Their glances passed from her, to the castle, and then back again. Their minds mused over those six hundred poor girls, lured away from the family table. So it now seemed, more apparent than ever, all for a rich woman's whim.

3. After hauling the sea turtle up in their nets, cutting it into pieces and roasting it, Jai and Joi discovered that it was Vishnu.

4. Every time Gaudentius cut himself, milk would spill from the wound. One day, while travelling, he passed through a village where the people were very hungry. He cut off his arm and filled all the vessels of the place with milk.

5. Few Houses Mountain has many houses.